CASSIE

Also available from the same author

THE WILDLIFE MAN

From a very young age, 'The Wildlife Man' loved and held a fascination with animals.
This is the story of how his passion for wildlife, originally a hobby, became first a part of his job as a police officer, then his full-time occupation and his life.
He is respected and admired for his work to this day. This is a heartfelt book, and the author's passion and appreciation for wildlife and nature is infectious.

Published by Upfront Publishing, 2002
ISBN 978-184426-026-3

Also available from the same author

RUNNING WILD

'Running Wild' is the story of a fox called Tarn who lived on the author's farm in the early 1950s, with steam trains on the LMS railway line, narrow boats trading on the Grand Union canal and 3,000 free-range chickens all on the farm.
Although this is a fictional story, some of the events described in the tale did occur and are seen through the eyes of Tarn.

Published by Upfront Publishing, 2005
ISBN 978-184426-327-4

Cassie

ISBN 978-184426-395-0

First Published 2006 by.
UPFRONT PUBLISHING LTD

Peterborough, England.

Printed by Print-on-Demand Worldwide Ltd.

CASSIE

BARRY KAUFMANN-WRIGHT

UPFRONT PUBLISHING
PETERBOROUGH, ENGLAND

This book is dedicated to
Marc Ashby
and Dave and Grace Kinnley

The Stories

The Early Days
The Vet
My First Walk
The Game
Dave and Grace
The Slipper
'Sam'
The Sea
The Police Office
The 'Mess' on the new carpet
The Cat
Rabbits
The Settee
The Police Car
Swimming
'Ace'
On The Beat
The Holiday
Fire!
The Rat and the Fox
The Cottage
The Prisoner
The Show
A Cooked Breakfast
The Swan
The Owl
The Kestrel
A 'Monster' in the sky
Goats
The Storm
Behind Bars
The Spiky Creature and the Fleas
'Chester'
The Canal
Snowed In
'Bismark'
The Rat
A New Addition to the family
Police Dogs!
The Downs
Snow and 'The Lads'
The Accident
A Problem in the Office
Three Men in a Wood
A Walk on the Motorway
The Snake
'Banjo'
Marc
New Surroundings
Cassie to the Rescue
A Romp on the Bed
The Deer
Hare Coursing
The Hunt
Life Goes On

Introduction

This is a story of a much loved Jack Russell Terrier by the name of 'Cassie', owned by the author. She lived for many years at the Police House at Thaxted in Essex where the author was the 'Village Bobby'. She was known and loved by many in the community.

She regularly accompanied the author on his patrols and was involved in all manner of incidents and adventures. The story is what happens through her eyes; Cassie is telling the story. All the events and incidents that she describes are true but some names have been changed.

All the photographs in this book are the work of the author, often with Cassie's assistance and participation.

She was a little dog with a big heart of gold, and a wonderful friend; the best friend a man could ever have or want.

CASSIE

The Early Days

I cannot remember much about my birth but I later learnt that I was one of six. My parents were named Jack and Jill. We were born in a house in a village called Tewin in Hertfordshire.

At about ten days' old my eyes opened for the first time. Initially all I could see was light and dark but as time went on all became clear. We grew fast and within a few weeks we became much more adventurous, exploring the small room that we were in from the cardboard box that was our home, and that had kept us secure when we were very young.

After a short while my brothers, sisters and I had made short work of reducing the walls of the box to a small sill, which meant we could hop out and explore. Mum remained with us all the time; her milk was lovely and we would squabble for the best position. We did not see much of dad, he would pop in occasionally with the humans but never stayed long.

The room we were in was small with only two wooden chairs, the legs of which tasted nice. The floor was covered in a smooth slippery surface which meant that when we tried to go faster our short legs would 'run' but we didn't go anywhere! But of course sense prevailed and we came up with the perfect solution: we started to chew it up. We began on the edges and worked towards the middle, it tasted revolting but it was good fun. There was a single light bulb hanging from the ceiling with a very dull light that was on all the time.

Mum and dad's human owners would come in regularly through the only door in the room. We would scamper for the safety of mum, but as the weeks went by she became a bit tetchy with us and would greet the humans with a wag of her stumpy tail and a yap of excitement that startled us. We all had stumpy tails as well, I do not recall losing mine, but I was still able to wag the stump.

One evening, when we were about six weeks old we were all resting, snuggled up to Mum after a hectic, boisterous game of tug of war with a piece of the flooring that we had ripped up. Suddenly the door opened and in came the woman with a couple who followed her into the room. The door closed and the three stood there looking at us. Mum got up to greet the woman, we followed. We sniffed cautiously at the man and woman who we had never seen before; I did not recognise their strange scent. The man was tall and had hair all over his face. The woman was a lot shorter and wore glasses. All three humans crouched down, not quite to our level but close. Suddenly the man reached out and picked me up in his huge hand, at the same time the woman with the glasses picked up my twin brother. I was a little unsure, I had only been picked up a couple of times and I didn't like it very much. They all stood up and I looked down the floor which was a long way away. The man then held me out with both his hands around me and my back legs just hanging there - it was most undignified. He seemed to be examining me, turning me this way and that. He then passed me to the woman with the glasses, who snuggled me close to her chin, I liked that! Eventually I was put back down and I scuttled back to mum. We played with the humans for a while and I think they liked me. They eventually left and we all snuggled up together and slept deeply; all the excitement had been too much.

Two weeks went by and life was fairly quiet. We played a lot and slept a lot. We had a few visitors but life generally was fairly uneventful. This was soon to change dramatically for me. Mum's milk was quickly drying up and we were being given bowls of real food, which heralded a lot of fighting between us as we competed for the delicious meals we were being offered. Mum's mood towards us also changed: she became less tolerant and kept snapping at us and giving us the occasional nip which was quite painful.

One evening we had all settled down after a particularly boisterous game of tag, when the door burst open and in came the woman with two other people, it was the man with the hair on his face and the woman with the glasses. We all ran up and greeted them; I got so excited I left a little puddle on the floor. My sister had run past the humans and out through the door onto the landing. She was chased by the woman, grabbed and brought back into the room. My sister and I had very similar markings. The man with the beard reached down and picked me up. He and the woman with the glasses made a real fuss of me. I licked her face and nearly knocked her glasses off. I licked the man and the hair on his face made me sneeze which made everyone laugh! We spent a long time playing and scampering around. Eventually the woman with the glasses picked me up and we left the room. That was the last time that I was to see my mum and the rest of the family, but my life's journey was beginning.

I was carried outside and the sunlight was quite bright. We got into a car and we left. I was sitting on the woman's lap, the man was driving. This was really exciting though the different scents confused me. The journey was really great, cradled in the woman's lap. Eventually we arrived at a house in Thaxted, which I was soon to learn was the 'Police House', although I didn't see the significance of this. I was carried into the house and placed in a plastic basket in the kitchen, an interesting place with some exciting scents. I was left alone which I did not like at all but I started to investigate the floor. Later the light was turned out and as I was worn out with all the excitement I curled up in my new bed and fell into a deep sleep.

I was awoken when the woman opened the door and walked in. I leapt out of my box to greet her and she caressed me, that was lovely but in my excitement I 'leaked' onto the floor. The woman, who became known to me as Lyn, gently picked me up and took me outside and placed me onto some strange stuff which I later learnt was 'grass' and the area was the 'garden'. She stood and watched me as I investigated.

The grass kept on tickling my nose and making me sneeze. The man – who was called Master - joined us with a cup in his hand. I ran up to him excitedly and leaked onto the grass (I am really going to have to control this!) In my excitement I knocked his hand holding the mug and spilt his tea.

Master and Lyn sat on a couple of logs by the shed door and watched me as I raced around taking in all the new and exciting scents, sights and sounds. Master reached down and picked me up then sat me on his lap. He cuddled me; his beard tickled my nose and I started sneezing uncontrollably which made the two of them laugh. They eventually went back indoors leaving me on the grass. They left the kitchen door open, but I couldn't climb up the steps so I sat at the bottom and whined; I didn't like being on my own. Master eventually appeared in some strange clothes which I later learnt was his police uniform. He picked me up and took me into the kitchen, then placed me into my basket. He walked down the hall and through a door which was closed behind him. This, I was to learn, was his office and a place where I was to meet a lot of people in years to come. I sat by the door and whined until Lyn picked me up and placed me in my basket under the worktop in the kitchen. This was the routine for a few weeks.

I soon settled in to my new home, and got on well with Master and Lyn. They fed me well which meant the 'wolf' in me didn't have to hunt! The garden was my domain and what an exciting place it was. Every morning there were new scents on the grass after the night's visitors.

The Vet

One morning Master and Lyn were up early and after my breakfast I was gathered up and placed in the car on Lyn's lap. We drove for a short while and then got out of the car. Lyn wouldn't put me down but carried me into a big building, Master followed. The air was full of interesting scents. We entered a room where there were a number of humans sitting down with a variety of animals of all shapes and sizes. I struggled to get down and go off and investigate but I was held firm. Sitting opposite us was a man with a huge dog with erect ears and a long shaggy coat. My view of the world was changed forever; I was not the only dog in the world!

The German Shepherd suddenly stood up as her Master stood. She had him on a lead and she led the way through a door into another room. As she passed me she sniffed me. Her head was bigger than my entire body; I thought that this must be the biggest dog in the world.

Eventually the door re-opened and the German Shepherd led her Master out, I remember thinking that she had trained her Master well. She had a very disgruntled look on her face and ignored me as they passed by and left. Master stood up and picked me up from Lyn's lap and we went into the room. Behind a shiny white table stood a tall man (The Vet) with hair on his face just like Master. As he took hold of me I realised that his hands were huge but gentle. He held me high in the air and looked at me all over, twisting me this way and that. I was not too sure about this but eventually I was placed down onto the table where I felt a lot happier. He then examined my ears, teeth, coat, paws, legs and even my rear end. I was rapidly going off this man!

Whilst this was going on Master and Lyn were talking to the vet. At one point he let go of me and this was my chance to escape but Master grabbed me and held me fast. Suddenly I felt a sharp pain in my thigh, I yelped in agony as the needle sank deep into my flesh. The vet rubbed it but that didn't help. Master picked me up and we left and we returned home. My thigh was sore for a few days. I decided that I didn't like the vet!

My First Walk

A few days after the visit to the vet, Lyn placed a leather collar around my neck; I didn't like it, and managed to remove it fairly quickly, only to have it put back on again, tighter this time. There was a small brass disc on the collar with the name 'Cassie' on it. This was the name that Master and Lyn had given me. Clipped to this collar was a long strip of leather called a lead. The back gate opened and I was led out into this new place, full of scents and things to investigate. This was my first time out into the big wide world.

In my struggles to go off and investigate I slipped the collar off but before I had chance to go off, Master's huge hands scooped me up and the collar was replaced, still tighter this time. I was desperate to go off and pulled and pulled until we reached the road at the front of the house. We started to walk along a path away from the house when suddenly a car sped past me; the breeze almost knocked me off my feet. I rushed to Lyn's legs and entwined the lead around her legs. Another car sped past and another, then a huge lorry that even towered over Master. I looked up at Lyn; I didn't like this at all. She picked me up and cradled me in her arms, I was safe again. Lyn stepped over the little puddle I had left on the path.

A short distance further along we left the road and began walking down a path with a tall hedge on one side and a field on the other. I was put down again; I could hear the cars in the distance but was more interested in the new scents and the hedge. I was still on the lead, despite my strongest efforts to get away. On and on we went, the sun was high in the sky and the hedge was full of bird song. At the bottom of the field we crossed a narrow lane with no cars and went over a bridge with water running underneath. This was the River Chelmer and was to become a place that I was to grow to love in the years to come.

After crossing the bridge we started to walk along the side of the river on a grass path. Suddenly Lyn leant down and unclipped the lead from my collar - I was free. I ran off so excitedly that I fell head over heels, Master and Lyn laughed at my misfortune, I was not amused. This was brilliant, investigating everything. Pushing my nose into holes in the top of the river bank, chasing curious things called butterflies. The water looked interesting but I wasn't allowed down the bank to investigate; the river was about three feet across but the water was running quite fast. There was a high hedge on the other side. There was so much to take in as we walked further and further along. The gentle breeze was bringing a multitude of different scents to my nostrils, and what with those and the myriad of sights and sounds, it was quite exhausting. Suddenly a bird flew out of the hedge and passed nearby me scalding as it did, it was a blackbird and I did not like it, I scampered back to Master, who stroked me reassuringly. I soon forgot about it and continued exploring.

We eventually left the river and walked up a field of grass to the church and the road. I made no objections when the lead was put back on. Master picked me up and we returned to the house with cars whooshing past us all the way back. Once we were safely back in the house I was put in a new basket in the kitchen and I went straight into a deep sleep, dreaming of my first walk. The cars, the scents, the river, the blackbird all came flashing back.

The Game

One morning after breakfast I was out on the back lawn when I was joined by Master, who was carrying a mug. He sat down on a log near the shed door and watched me. I came over to him, sat on his foot and chewed his slipper. He shooed me away but I ran back and did it again. He placed his mug down, picked me up in his huge hands and held me up to his face and we stared at each other. He was smiling at me.

He placed me down on the lawn, I scampered off running flat out in tight circles, ending in a rush at Master and colliding with his legs. He walked over onto the lawn and sat down on the grass. I started running around him. He tried to grab me but missed. I jumped over his outstretched legs and almost fell over when I landed. Around and around I ran as fast as my little legs would carry me, this was great fun. Master grabbed me and held me high in the air as he lay down on the grass. I wriggled desperately to get away and he put me down. I ran around him again, jumping over his face at one end and his legs at the other. Lyn had joined us and was watching from the log. Master sat up and on his knees he started to chase me around and around. At one point I ran through his legs, he tried to grab me but I was too quick for him.

He was laughing hysterically as we dodged past each other, this really was great fun. He eventually grabbed me. I let him catch me and I was held high in the sky as he lay down again. I looked down on his face below me, he was smiling at me. He slowly lowered me down onto his chest and let go of me. I licked his face all over as he tried to brush me away. I jumped off his chest, over his head and started running again. Master stood up and I ran around his legs in a tight circle again. I tried to rush in once or twice to nip his slipper but missed on both occasions. On one 'attack' he caught me and lifted me up; I wriggled so much that he nearly dropped me. He sat down on the log next to Lyn, and I sat on his lap. I was panting heavily after all this exercise. I spotted his mug next to the log so I wriggled to get down, he didn't know why. I got down and while he and Lyn were talking, I heard my name mentioned, I crept around to the mug and started drinking the cold tea within; it tasted quite nice. There was not a lot in there and as I tried to reach the last drop in the bottom the mug suddenly fell over and smashed. Master looked down and said something which I did not understand but the tone suggested that I had done something wrong. I scampered off as he stood up. I thought the game was on again and started running around him but he was not playing. He disappeared into the house only to reappear shortly after with a dustpan and brush. As he swept up the remains of the mug, I had my eye on the brush which I had seen before and which I was really interested in. I tried to grab it but Master sent me away. I scuttled back and tried to grab it again but Master had finished sweeping.

Dave and Grace

As the weeks went by we got into a routine, which I loved. As soon as Master or Lyn came down the stairs I was let out into the garden. Then I was back in, still having difficulty with the steps by the kitchen door. After my breakfast, which I really enjoyed, I was placed on my lead and I walked excitedly along the road as we accompanied Phil to school.

One morning when we were walking as usual, we were passing the end of a garden when I saw a huge man standing in the garden. Master spoke to him and I crawled through the hedge to introduce myself. The man, whose name I was to learn was Dave, reached down and picked me up; I was smothered by his huge hands. He held me up to his chin and I licked his face. He didn't have a beard like Master but his face was really rough where he hadn't shaved. He carried me down the path of his garden and through the open back door where I met a lady, Dave's wife Grace. Grace gave me a little treat, a biscuit, which was delicious. Master dropped Phil off at school and returned to the garden. Dave brought me out, still holding me in his hands and put me down. I ran over to Master and we walked home. I was to grow to love Dave and Grace, and their biscuits, in the years that followed.

The Slipper

A few weeks after meeting Dave and Grace, I was left on my own one morning in the kitchen, as Master and Lyn had gone out. I was tired after my early morning walk taking Gina to school and I slept for quite a while. I was awoken by the phone ringing but of course there was no one around to answer it and it soon stopped ringing. On the floor in the kitchen was a pair of slippers which bore the strong scent of Master.

I pushed my nose into one of them and as I did so it started to slide across the floor, this was fun. I couldn't see where I was going and bumped into something solid which startled me. I pulled my head out to see what I had hit, it was the back door. I pushed my head deep into the slipper and travelled further around the room until I came to an abrupt halt again - this time it was the cooker, then the fridge, and the other door. Eventually I got bored with this and flicked the slipper into the air; it came down on my head! I did this a few more times then, pretending it was something to kill, I pounced on it and bit hard into the rubber sole, it had a strange taste.

I then had a rough and tumble with the slipper, rolling over and over with it held firmly in my mouth. I lay on my back with the slipper on my chest, held by my front paws. I proceeded to tear at the rubber and it came off in tiny little pieces, this was great fun. In no time at all the floor and I were covered in rubber. The smaller pieces got up my nose and made me sneeze.

When all the rubber had been removed from the slipper I turned my attention to the material on top. This was interesting, it was very stringy and kept getting stuck in my teeth, I used my front paws to remove it. Soon there was very little of the slipper left and I was tired. I crawled into my basket and slept only to be awoken soon after by the sound of a car in the rear yard. I leapt out of my basket and skidded on all the debris on the floor. I stood at the door wagging my tail and barking excitedly as I saw Lyn's outline through the glass.

The door opened and in came Lyn. I jumped up to greet her, but as she came in she looked at the floor and said "Oh no" and she looked at me. Master followed her in and I greeted him but he looked at the floor and said to me "You bad girl", I was soon to learn what this term meant by the tone of Lyn and Master's voices. I had obviously done something wrong, so I skulked back to my basket. Master picked up the shredded remains of his slipper, waved it close to my face and said "What is this?" By the tone of his voice I was obviously in trouble. I looked up at him in a pathetic way and he said "You bad, bad girl". He then threw the remains into the bin and Lyn swept up all the debris. I don't really know what all the fuss was about, he had the other slipper!

'Sam'

Late one afternoon, Lyn placed me in the car and we were soon off on our travels. I sat across Phil and Gina's laps and I slept for a while until the car stopped. We all got out onto a large patch of grass with houses behind. We called at one of the houses where there was a strong smell of cat on the doorstep. A man came to the door whom I recognised as Martin, I had met him before at the police house. We went in and the air was full of the scent of cat. Andrea was in the kitchen cooking. We went through to the sitting room and Master let me off my lead.

I sat on Lyn's lap as everyone was talking. Martin came over and picked me up and sat me on his lap. I licked his face and he laughed which made me want to lick him more. Suddenly I saw a white head with long whiskers appear through the top banister of the stairs. I barked and leapt off Martin's lap to investigate. I ran along the hall and rushed up the stairs. Master and Martin shouted at me but I ignored them. The cat was at the top of the stairs and it ran into the bedroom, I ran after it. I followed it up onto the bed but it jumped off and ran out of the door. I chased after it, down the stairs we rushed and through Master's legs - he tried to catch me but he missed. Master shouted again but for some reason I didn't hear him! This was a great game, although I do not think that the cat thought so.

We ran into the sitting room and around the chairs with everyone trying to catch me, I was too quick for them all. We dashed back along the hall, up the stairs and back onto the bed. The cat leapt off again but dived under the bed. I went to follow but was startled when I was confronted by a spitting, snarling, fierce cat. I jumped back and barked; the cat seized the initiative and darted at me. I ran off and dived between Master's legs (he was standing in the doorway of the bedroom) and back down the stairs with the cat close behind me. I leapt onto Lyn's lap and the cat was about to follow, but stopped at Andrea's feet. Andrea grabbed the cat with both hands and carried it through to the kitchen and shut the door. It was then that I learnt that the cat's name was 'Sam'.

Later in the evening everyone was sitting at the table eating and I was underneath waiting for any morsels when I suddenly saw Sam through the glass windows, she was in the garden. I barked and rushed at the glass and hit it hard. Sam ran off whilst I was left with a very sore nose. I didn't see her again that day but our paths were to cross frequently in the future.

The Sea

As I grew older and more mature, Master and I would go on longer and longer walks through the beautiful countryside around Thaxted, and Dave would often join us. There were a lot of exciting sights, scents and sounds to discover everywhere.

When we went out in the car my favourite place was on the back shelf under the rear window where I could see everything. Being small, I could fit onto the shelf quite easily. It was difficult sometimes when the car braked sharply as I would sometimes slip off the shelf down onto the seat, only to jump back up again. The world is huge! Loads of scents came into the car from food to cats, dogs and of course to humans, it was all very confusing.

Early one morning Lyn gave me my food as usual and I went out into the garden. There was a very strong, musty scent in a couple of places on the lawn. A fox had been in the garden overnight and had marked his territory. Lyn gathered me up and placed me on the back seat where Phil joined me. I jumped up onto the back shelf, the sun was just coming up when we left.

We were travelling for a long time and I fell asleep. When I woke up I wanted the toilet so I started to whine. Master stopped on the side of a busy road, my lead was put on and I was taken to a patch of grass that was so full of interesting scents that I forgot about my toilet - that was until Master started tugging on my lead, and by the tone of his voice he was getting angry, so I did my toilet and I was placed back into the car.

We eventually arrived at a town with some very strange scents and one in particular seemed to dominate the air. We stopped at a house and we all got out. There were a number of large white birds flying around in the blue sky with their arms outstretched, calling loudly. I didn't like them and kept close to Lyn's legs as we went into the house. I recognised the scents and the voices of the two women in the house; they were similar to Master's. I wanted to go off and investigate but was prevented by my lead. However after a short while I was bundled back into the car with everyone. We were a bit squashed in the back so I sat on Phil's lap. After a short distance we stopped and we all got out. Then I discovered where the dominant scent was coming from. There in front of me was a huge expanse of water with big waves crashing down near us. This, I was to learn was the sea.

I was really excited and as soon as my lead was taken off I ran off down to the water but then a huge wave crashed down right in front of me, white, wild and foaming. The water then raced up towards me, scaring the living daylights out of me and I ran back to the group who were laughing at me. I hid behind Master's legs. He reached down, picked me up and cradled me in his arms whilst I hid my head in his armpit as he carried me towards the water. I felt safe in his arms.

I was carried along the water's edge and eventually curiosity got the better of me and I poked my head out to see what was happening. Master put me down, I wasn't too certain about this and kept close to Master as the waves continued to crash down. The strong wind was blowing the spray onto us, the water tasted funny.

Eventually we reached a long construction that went out into the sea; Master picked me up and told me that this was Worthing Pier. Of course I understood exactly what he meant, but all I was interested in was getting away from the waves. Still on my lead we walked up onto the pier, this was really strange. I could see the sea through the gaps between the wooden slats that made up the floor and I wasn't too sure about this. My paws kept slipping through the gaps. I soon learnt to tread carefully!

There was a strong breeze blowing across the pier as we walked along. A number of people were sitting on benches as we continued down. My attention was regularly distracted by the smell of food, especially my favourite, fish and chips, but Master kept me tight on the lead. However I did get one chip when a seagull flew over carrying a beak full of chips. He was being mobbed by other gulls and dropped a chip right in front of me. I grabbed it before anyone saw, it was delicious.

At the end of the pier we all sat down and looked out. I sat on the lady's lap so that I could see, mind you the view was pretty unimpressive, just water as far as the eye could see! While we sat there several people walked past with dogs on leads, one was a very handsome Jack Russell. I wanted to meet him but I was held firm, it wasn't fair!

Eventually I was put down and we started walking back down the pier. I could still taste the chip in my mouth and I tried to grab another that was under one of the seats but the harder I strained, the harder Master pulled me back, it just wasn't fair. We went back to the house where everyone sat around talking, and I got bored. However, eventually I was bundled into the car and we returned home. I slept for most of the journey, dreaming about the sea and the pier, two places that I was to grow fond of later in my life.

The Police Office

Almost every day, Master would disappear through a door into a room attached to the house, which I was to learn was the 'police office'. Initially I was not allowed in there. One morning Master went into the office and Lyn had gone out in the car. The kitchen and the office door were both open so I crept into the office. Master was sitting at a big desk and did not see me immediately.

Suddenly there was a loud knock at the outside office door. I barked. I could see a person standing outside through the glass. I continued barking to tell Master that there was someone there. He walked over to the door, scooped me up, and the person came in and spoke to Master. I continued barking until Master spoke to me rather firmly. This was a situation that I was to become accustomed to.

After this person left Master sat down at his desk and placed me on his lap. I climbed up with my front feet on his chest and licked his face. His beard tickled my nose and made me sneeze uncontrollably. The phone rang and Master placed me down onto the carpet. I went off and explored every nook and cranny of the office. It was an interesting room. In addition to Master's desk and chair, there was a long counter which stretched virtually the full width of the room, with a small door at one end.

As a result of the counter the scents in the office were quite interesting, for on the side where Master sat at his desk the scents on the floor were his and Lyn's but on the other side there was a real mixture where other people had come and gone. The office was a room that I was to grow to love and where I was to spend a lot of time, either with Master or just looking out of the glass door to the path and road beyond. This was the only door in the house where I could look out on the great wide, busy and exciting world outside. If Master was sitting at his desk I would lay on his feet, even though he was in his uniform he always had his slippers on, and they were soft and warm!

The mess on the new carpet

I soon learnt to do my 'toilet' outside and only had accidents when I got really excited, then I would 'leak' slightly. One evening, I was taking Master for a walk when we called at a house near the Church. I was introduced to the couple, who I liked. While Master sat talking to them I was allowed to go off and investigate some interesting scents. The carpet was new. It was lovely and soft under my feet. In the kitchen I found some crumbs on the floor, they were delicious, and I searched for more.

Eventually I heard Master call "Cassie, where are you?" I scampered over to him and my lead was put on. We walked along a passageway towards the front door when suddenly the man said to Master "Look what your dog has done on our new carpet", he indicated an apparent pile of 'pooh' right near the front door. Master looked down at me and shouted in a tone which I knew meant I was in deep trouble. My head went down and I rolled over. Master dragged me up to this huge pile by the door, pointed at it and scolded me again. I didn't know what I had done, it wasn't mine. I went over to it and sniffed it. It wasn't pooh, it was plastic. The man and woman were laughing out loud. The man reached down and picked the pooh up in his fingers. Master burst into laughter, reached down and picked me up, and caressed me, hugging and apologising to me. The man gave me a biscuit. I didn't quite understand what was going on, but I enjoyed the treat. It may have been a joke pooh but I didn't think it was very funny.

The Cat

One morning I was walking Master and we were taking Phil to school. On reaching the end of Dave and Grace's garden I was let off my lead and I ran down the path towards their back door. The hedge on one side had been trimmed and on the other there were some tall plants that Dave called broccoli. I ran down excitedly when suddenly a huge black monster leapt out of the broccoli to my side. Startled, I ran even faster but the monster jumped up onto my back, its needle-like claws sank deep into my head and back. I yelped loudly in pain and fear as the cat tried to claw at my eyes.

Master was running down the path shouting at the cat. At the same time the kitchen door opened and I saw Dave rushing out. I ran towards him and at the last minute the cat leapt off me and disappeared as quickly as it had appeared through the hedge. I hid behind Dave, shaking and shivering. My back was really sore and blood was running down my face. Dave reached down and swept me up in his huge hands, cradling me in his arms. Master checked me over and swabbed the spots that were bleeding. I was shaking uncontrollably.

Master carried me home and I was bundled straight into the car where I shivered on Lyn's lap while Master drove. To make things worse I was taken to the dreaded vet, where I was prodded and poked around and had the inevitable injection in my rump, I do not like vets but hate cats even more. My wounds took a while to heal but my dislike of cats never improved.

Rabbits

One morning after breakfast Master backed the car out of the garage, and I watched through a crack in the fence. I got excited, were we going out? Lyn and the kids came out of the kitchen door, and she closed it behind her. They all went out through the gate and I followed. I jumped into the car and immediately up onto the back window shelf, my favourite place. Phil and Gina were in the back with me. I licked both their ears, just to let them know that I was there!

We travelled for a long time. I slept for most of the journey, dreaming, until I was awoken suddenly by a strong, familiar scent. It was the smell of the sea, we were back at Worthing. We stayed at the house for a while as Master, Lyn and the others sat around talking and drinking tea. Eventually we all got in the car and drove for a short while up to The Downs. We got out and the air was fresh and full of scent. There were some curious animals with thick woolly coats in the field next to where we had parked. I heard Master refer to these as 'sheep' and to this place as 'Cissbury Ring'. We climbed up the hill with a strong wind in our faces, it was lovely. I was running all over the place investigating all the new scents. There were no sheep on the hill but their droppings were everywhere.

The sun was shining down and there wasn't a cloud in the sky. Birds were singing high above us. I had heard them at Thaxted and believe they were called 'skylarks'. The sheep had young and the air was full of their bleating below us. What a fabulous place this was, there was so much to take in. We reached the top and started to walk around.

I suddenly spotted a rabbit sitting up looking at me a few yards ahead - I gave chase. It disappeared down a nearby hole in the ground and I chased down the hole after it. More fun!

After the bright sunlight it was really dark and cool down in the tunnel. The scent of the rabbit was strong and I could hear it scampering along way ahead of me. The chase was on, what fun. Down and down I went; the soil was interesting, it was white and quite slippery. Eventually I came to a side tunnel which went off from the one I was in, the scent was strong from this one so I turned off and continued. The tunnels were huge with smooth white sides and roofs and I had no trouble.

Apart from the noise I was making it was very quiet down in the tunnels compared to all the sounds and the wind outside. I came to a crossroads of tunnels with passages going off in all directions, but I was confused as there were scents in all of them. Suddenly I heard a scuffling sound from way down a tunnel to my side so I went off again. I had chosen the right one for the scent was rapidly growing stronger. The tunnel was dropping down at quite a steep angle but I didn't care as I descended deeper and deeper into the bowels of the hill. Suddenly the tunnel I was in came to an abrupt end with a huge piece of flintstone blocking the path. But all was not lost for there was a tunnel leading off to a side. I continued on for a short distance before the tunnel opened up into a large chamber, I lost my balance and fell onto the floor which was covered in dry grass. Although there were no rabbits there, in amongst the dry grass there was a lot of rabbit fur and the scent was very strong. There were a number of tunnels leading off this chamber. I sat for a moment getting my breath and listening intently, but it was very quiet, there was not a sound from any of the tunnels.

With the strong scents all around me I couldn't make up my mind which tunnel to take but eventually I scrambled up and chose one and I ran along it for quite a while. I came to a side tunnel and turned into it, then almost immediately I heard the very faint sound of Master calling my name. By the tone of his voice he sounded anxious so I barked a reply. The tunnel I was in went into a steep incline; it was hard going with my short stumpy legs, but then the tunnel levelled off. Master's voice was still very faint.

Eventually I came to another crossroads in the tunnels. There was fresh air blowing along one of the tunnels so I followed that one and suddenly I was on the surface, the bright sunlight dazzling me momentarily. I shook myself and looked around for Master, who I could see some way away.

He was down on his hands and knees with his head and shoulders out of sight down the tunnel that I had run down. His backside was sticking up in the air! I shook myself again and ran over to him. I crawled down the tunnel beside him - this was a great game. I licked his face and he jumped in surprise. With some difficulty he pulled himself out of the tunnel and sat on the grass. He picked me up and hugged me then brushed me down with his hand, the chalk came off me in clouds. He sat and talked to me for quite a while and although I hadn't got a clue what he was talking about the tone suggested to me that I had done something wrong, but I couldn't think what! Eventually we walked off side by side. I kept looking up at him; he hadn't realised that his face was filthy and he had chalk and dirt in his hair, beard and all over his clothes!

We joined the others who were sitting on a bench at the top of the hill. They all started laughing at us as we approached, I couldn't think why but Master was covered in dirt and chalk. We eventually walked down the hill back to the car. Later in the day we set off for Thaxted and I slept all the way home on the back shelf dreaming about rabbits and tunnels!

The Settee

I was to learn early on in my life that certain places in the house were 'no go' areas and one of these was the settee in the sitting room. I had sneaked up on to it once or twice, which was no mean feat as it was so high, only to be ousted most unceremoniously by either Master or Lyn.

Sometimes, however, if either of them were on their own in the evening, with Master on duty or Lyn out dancing, I was allowed up to keep them company. I would snuggle down between them and the arm of the settee. It was lovely and warm there and I would soon fall off to sleep and dream.

When I woke up I would sit bolt upright using the back of the seat as a support and lick the face of whoever I was sitting next to. Master's beard would tickle my nose and make me sneeze. I did love being spoilt!

When whoever was out came in I was gently lifted off the settee onto my beanbag bed in front of the television.

Master would often come in with my friend David when they were both in uniform. After a cup of tea and a chat they were off out again. Master was the village policeman for Thaxted. David was his assistant, and they were often on duty in the evenings.

The Police Car

One evening Master was in uniform sitting in his office. Lyn had gone up the long flight of steps which I didn't like. They were wooden and highly polished and I had slipped and fallen on them a couple of times which hurt. I was all on my own downstairs. The office door between the house and the office was shut but I could hear Master behind the door. I sat and whined loudly until Master opened the door and let me in; I knew it would work.

After checking that it was safe for Master to be in there, I curled up on his feet and went to sleep. Shortly after this Master made a move to get up and I woke with a start from a deep sleep. He stood up and gathered up some papers off his desk and walked to the front door. I watched him as the door opened and he went outside. Suddenly he called me and I scampered outside, it was dark. We walked around to the rear yard where the car with the funny roof lights and bright markings down the side was parked. This was the 'police car'. Master opened the door and ushered me in. This was the first time that I had been in the police car. I climbed up on to the back shelf but there was not as much room on this one as there was in the other car. A lot of the space was taken up by some sort of long roll, which I was later to learn was a roller blind saying 'Police Stop'. This was operated by a long cord that extended from the blind along the roof to the front where Master sat. It was most inconvenient having that on the shelf but I managed to squeeze in.

We set off. The radio in the front was different to the one in the other car. A person would talk and then there was a long period of bleeps, very strange. We travelled a short while and then Master stopped the car in a car park. I jumped out when Master opened the door and I had a quick toilet. We then went into the building which Master told me was Saffron Walden Police Station. It was full of interesting scents. I wandered all over the building whilst Master sat talking and drinking tea with three other men in the same uniform.

I was in one of the offices upstairs when I heard Master calling me. I ran down the stairs and in my enthusiasm I nearly fell. We left the building and got back into the car, I jumped up onto the shelf. We were driving around the countryside quite slowly and Master told me that this was 'patrolling' but I hadn't got a clue what he was on about as usual. All I did know was that I enjoyed it. We eventually came up behind a car that was travelling along very slowly. We passed it and then the roof lights started flashing brightly, I could see the flashing in the hedge next to us. Master pulled the string and the roller blind went up displaying the words 'Police Stop'. We slowed down and the other car did the same. After we had stopped Master got out and told me to "stay". I watched out of the back window but could see very little because of the lights of the car behind and the flashing of our roof lights.

Eventually Master got back into the car and spoke briefly on the radio, and then he wrote something down. He got out and went to the car behind, only to return again soon, and we drove off. I jumped down from the shelf and squeezed through the gap between the two front seats to sit on the passenger seat. I licked Master's hand. He told me that I was a good girl and explained to me that he had stopped the car for a 'routine stop check' of course I fully understood what he meant? I licked his hand again.

We 'patrolled' for quite a while and then returned to the police house and bed. With all the excitement I was really tired. Master said, “Goodnight Cassie” and he went up the stairs. I curled up in my bed and went into a deep sleep. The evening excursions with Master in the police car were to become a regular feature of my life and I would get really excited if I saw Master in his uniform in the evenings, as I knew we were off on another adventure.

Swimming

As the spring stretched into my first summer, the days got hotter and longer and our evening 'patrols' were no longer in the dark. I could see so much more. Lyn and Master would take me on some fantastic walks after we had taken Phil to school and Gina to playgroup, and I had eaten my biscuit at Dave and Grace's. One of my favourite walks was along the River Chelmer.

One evening we had a very bad storm, the flashes and the loud cracks of thunder terrified me. Master had been called out on an emergency. Lyn came down the stairs and into the kitchen. She could see me trembling so she reached down and picked me up and sat me on her lap on the settee in the sitting room. There was a very loud crack of thunder that sounded as if it was directly above us. I crawled down beside Lyn, hiding my head. Lyn stroked my back reassuringly, which was beautiful, and we later fell asleep in the warmth, side by side. We were awoken the following morning by Master returning; it was daylight and the storm had gone.

The lawn was very wet. After Master had fed we took the kids to their respective schools and I had my biscuit at Dave and Grace's, being careful as I passed the broccoli plants that towered over me. We then went for a walk down the field track next door to us and along to the river which was really high after all the rain last night. I had never seen it like this before. We crossed the little footbridge; the torrential water just below the boards.

On reaching the path on the other side I ran on ahead of Master. The air was clear and fresh and the sun was already high in the sky. A strong, interesting scent reached my nostrils and seemed to be coming from the remaining river bank that wasn't under water. I climbed down the bank and suddenly saw a water vole just slightly ahead of me. Almost instantly it jumped into the water and disappeared. I rushed forward and in my excitement I lost my footing and fell into the rushing water. I sank momentarily only to resurface immediately afterwards. Using my legs I 'swam' across to the other side and pulled myself out, not without some difficulty, as the rushing water tried to pull me back in. I shook myself and looked across at Master. I had a quick look around at the bank and in the undergrowth but there was no sign of the vole. Master called me back so I jumped into the swirling water and swam across but I was swept downstream quite a way before I emerged back with Master.

I shook myself and the water cascaded over him before I led him off along the path. This water was really great fun and I had several more swims on that walk, but did not see anything more of the vole. I was reluctant to leave the river but we eventually returned home. I slept blissfully for the remainder of the day, so did Master. Lyn had gone out in the car.

On the Beat

Late one evening, Master was in the sitting room in uniform talking to Lyn. He eventually got up and went through to the office and I followed - I was not going to miss anything. I got really excited when Master put my lead on. He then took his helmet off the counter and put it on. I jumped up on his leg in excitement and he patted me on the head. We then left the office and went out into the dark, mild night air.

We walked up onto the recreation ground where Master let me off my lead, there were some interesting scents in the hedgerows. We walked right around the recreation ground before my lead was put back on then we walked through a gap into a small estate of houses. There were street lights here and the bases of these lights were covered in interesting scents. All was quiet on this estate and we walked on to an alley, which leads to the school.

As we walked up the alley I could hear voices ahead and we came upon a group of young men standing in the shadows. Master spoke to them and we then walked on. I turned around to see where the men were but they were gone. We reached the school and Master shone his torch through the gate railings at the school buildings. Seeing nothing of concern we continued and eventually arrived in Town Street where we walked up one side and back down the other, Master was checking the doors of all the shops.

From there we walked down Park Street where Master checked the doors of the doctors' surgery and a few other doors before walking back up through Town Street, past the Guildhall and into Stoney Lane, which was difficult for me to walk on with the cobble stones, but eventually we arrived on the smooth path in the churchyard. In the silence of the night I could hear giggling coming from the church porch. We walked across the grass towards the porch - I was straining at the lead to investigate but Master held me firm.

When we reached the porch Master switched his torch on and a very startled young couple looked at us from a bench within the porch. The girl was partially dressed and she very quickly put her clothes back on. Master spoke to them and they quickly got up and walked off, saying "Goodnight Officer" to Master as they left. Master and I walked all around the church checking all the doors.

We then walked down a path to the windmill where I was let off my lead. There were some interesting scents including a strong scent of a fox that had passed through quite recently. I started to follow this scent but Master called me back. He was leaning on a fence and it was very quiet and still, the only sound was a distant owl hooting.

From the windmill we walked back past the church and eventually into the main car park where a few cars were parked. Master shone his torch into the windscreen of all the cars - he appeared to be checking something - and wrote down the details of two of the cars. From there we walked into a large estate of houses where more cars were parked. Master checked all the cars and wrote down on a pad the details of some of the cars. As we were about to leave the estate I heard the sound of a car approaching very slowly. Master slipped the looped end of my lead over a low fence post, I was held firm. As the car approached Master moved out into the road and raised his arm above his head. The car stopped in front of him. The driver got out of his car and Master spoke to him for some time before producing a gadget from his pocket and assembling it. The man then breathed into the gadget while I watched as a small bag filled up. Master then looked at the gadget with his torch and spoke to the man again. He got back into his car and drove off.

We came out of the estate and were walking towards the recreation ground when I heard voices ahead of us; Master shortened my lead. We stopped for a moment and the voices appeared to be coming from some bushes ahead of us. We walked on and suddenly Master switched his torch on - the beam highlighted two young men sitting under the hedge with bottles in their hands. They appeared very startled as they got unsteadily to their feet. Master spoke to them for quite a while and they tipped the contents of their bottles out under the hedge before staggering off past us and onto the estate. Master stood and watched them for some time until they disappeared into one of the houses.

We then walked back home through the recreation ground and I curled up in my basket going into a deep sleep. I was to accompany Master on a number of his late night 'foot patrols' around Thaxted over the years and I always enjoyed myself.

'Ace'

A family who visited the house fairly regularly and whom I grew to love were Kath and John, and their two children Marc and Faith. Sometimes they would stay for a few days, which was great fun.

Early one morning I heard a car arrive in the back yard and I recognised the engine sound as being that of John and Kath's car. I whined at the kitchen door to be let out. I was so excited I 'leaked' slightly on the lino. Lyn opened the door and I ran out to the gate. Through the gap in the fence I could see Kath, John and the kids getting out of the car and what a surprise I had when I saw John holding a black and white Jack Russell puppy in his arms. I barked in excitement. They passed through the gate, which was closed carefully behind them. John then placed the puppy down on the lawn. I sniffed him all over - he smelt strange - and he sniffed me. Master, John and the others watched us for a while and then left us alone and went inside. The puppy's name was Ace and he was slightly older than me. He was black and white and all muscle, his eyes were bright and deep, he was very handsome.

We investigated each other very closely and then started playing, chasing each other round and round on the grass, falling over each other. This was really great fun especially as I didn't get much time to play with any friends. We ran and ran until eventually we dropped down on the grass to catch our breaths. We sat looking at each other until I caught a movement out of the corner of my eye and looked up to see John and Lyn looking through the window at us. The sun was high in the sky and we just lay there soaking up the warmth until the kitchen door opened. Master, John, Marc and Phil appeared on the lawn and Master was holding my lead. That could only mean one thing, we were off for a walk (or as Master would often say to Lyn in code a 'Whiskey, Alpha, Lima, Kilo'). They thought I would not understand that but I soon cottoned on to what it meant.

We walked along the river bank; it was beautiful. Ace and I played and investigated the scents along the path. Master and John were in deep conversation, while Phil and Marc were behind, talking. The wind was gently brushing through the trees which were full of bird song. Ace and I ran on ahead, Ace was faster than me, but we both stopped abruptly as we heard a plop in the water and saw ripples coming out from the water's edge below us. We both chased down the bank and on reaching the water we dived in to chase the water vole which had long gone by now. The water was lovely and cool and refreshing. We soon forgot about the vole and swam across to the other side. We pulled ourselves out, shook the water off and checked out a few scents before re-entering the water. Master and John were sitting on the other bank watching us. We swam over to them ran up the bank and shook ourselves right next to them. The water cascaded over them, we were not popular! We eventually returned home the way we had come. I curled up in my box; I was tired after all the excitement of the day and Ace curled up with me. Much later Ace was collected by John and they left.

The following morning I was out on the lawn and Ace's scent was everywhere, I missed him, but it wasn't long before we were to meet up again. Early one morning I was bundled into the car and Lyn and the kids followed. I sat up on the back shelf and soon went to sleep. It was a long journey but eventually we arrived at a house and as I leapt out there were some familiar scents, including that of Ace. The front door of the house opened and there stood John and Kath. I ran up to them and greeted them, and in my excitement I left a little 'puddle' on the path.

Once in the house I could hear Ace behind the kitchen door which Kath then opened. We greeted each other excitedly; Kath stepped over us and walked through the door. We ran out into the garden and played for ages. Eventually Master and John came out with leads in their hands and they were fixed to our collars. We were led out through a side gate to the front of the house where all the others were waiting.

We walked though the small estate, down a short path and out into open fields, where our leads were removed. Marc, Faith, Phil and Gina were walking ahead of the others. We ran past them at full pace, this was great fun. Eventually we reached a huge expanse of water. It was so big I could not see the other side. The clear blue sky was reflected on the still surface. The sun was really hot and with all the running around I was quite hot so I leapt into the water, which was lovely and cool. Ace followed me in and we swam right out for no particular reason apart from the joy of swimming, which I for one love.

When I looked back at Master, Lyn and the others a strange sight greeted me. Phil and Marc were taking their clothes off down to what I now know to be their trunks. They then both waded into the water and swam up to us. Master and the others were standing laughing at the sight in front of them. There were Marc and Phil swimming side by side with Ace and me between them. We swam out to a small shallow island where we all climbed out of the water. It was warm in the sun after the coolness of the water. The boys sat there for a while talking. They then went back into the water and swam around the island splashing each other and laughing. Ace and I joined in as much as we could, I was chasing Marc and Ace was chasing Phil, it was great fun.

Eventually we all swam back to the bank where the others were sitting on the grass. Ace and I were reluctant to come out of the water but eventually we were persuaded to. I ran up to Lyn and shook myself, she laughed as she dried herself off. The rest of the walk took us right around the large lake which I learnt was part of the flood meadows of the River Nene at Rushden, Northampton. There were many interesting scents, particularly of other dogs and rabbits. Back at the house, Ace and I dried off on the lawn where the others joined us with a cup of tea.

Later in the day we all got into the cars and drove a short distance to a pub where we sat out in the back garden. There was a little stream at the end of this garden, which I for one wanted to investigate but I was on my lead, as was Ace. Master and the others had a meal there. Both Ace and I sat under the table ready to catch anything that might fall off, but nothing did! We stayed in the pub garden for most of the afternoon, it was really hot. We were given a bowl of cool water to drink and it was refilled three times, we were really thirsty.

We returned to Thaxted very late in the day. I slept on Phil's lap all the way home, I was really tired after all the excitement of the day and dreamt of swimming and of Ace.

The Holiday

It was the time of the year when the kids were on holiday from school. This meant no walks down to Dave and Grace's in the morning but we called in on them in the evening instead.

One morning things were set to change. I had sensed an air of excitement in the house over the past few days. This morning everybody got up really early, it was still dark outside. Master, Phil and Lyn were packing cases and bags into the back of the car. Even my basket was packed which caused me a lot of concern. Lyn tried to explain to me that we were 'going on holiday' whatever that meant. Eventually we got into the car and set off. I was sitting on Phil's lap for a while but eventually went to sleep on the back shelf; from here I could lick Phil and Gina's ears, which made them giggle. I slept for quite a while, as did Phil and Gina. When I awoke it was daylight and we were just pulling off the road into what Master called a 'service station'. We parked behind another car out of which stepped John and Kath. I got really excited and jumped down onto Phil's lap, he gave out a groan. I was just squeezing through to the front seat when Master and Lyn got out and slammed the doors. I watched them all from the windscreen but I could not see Ace. They were soon back in the car and we were off, following John and Kath's car. As we pulled back onto the road I suddenly saw Ace's face in the back window of their car.

I slept on Lyn's lap, this was a long journey. We continued on for quite a while until we pulled off the road again into a pub. Lyn put my lead on and I was out like a shot. I pulled Lyn over to see the other car and Ace leapt out, also on his lead. We greeted each other with wagging tails and sniffing. I was really pleased to see him. We had a bowl of water, which we shared, and a biscuit each.

It was a beautiful, sunny, warm day and everyone sat at a table outside and had a bite to eat. Ace and I chased around the grass area. Later we were back in the cars and off on our long journey. We soon pulled off the main road and were travelling along a winding road which seemed to go on forever. The smell of the sea was wafting into the car. Eventually we pulled off the lane into a grass field where a few strange houses on wheels were parked up. We pulled alongside one huge one and stopped. Lyn put my lead back on and we were out. I joined Ace in investigating the interesting scents including strong ones of sheep.

The cars were unloaded into the unusual house which I later learnt was a 'caravan'. Ace and I went inside to investigate but it was more interesting outside and we were soon out running around on our own. Much later we took Master and John for a long walk. We went out of the field and along a long track which went down to the sea and finished at a sandy beach. John told us that this was called 'Whistling Sands'. Ace and I ran along the beach, chasing each other. The sand was so soft it eased up between our pads, which made running hard work. We were soon joined by Lyn, Kath and the others. The sun was setting and there was a gentle breeze blowing. Small waves were lapping on the shore as we left the beach and walked back along the track to the caravan. The kids were soon in bed at one end, giggling and laughing, until Master told them to be quiet. Soon after that everyone else was in bed too. Ace and I had our separate beds on the floor in the kitchen area but as everyone settled down for the night, Ace crept out of his bed and snuggled up with me, he was nice and warm. Various sounds of snoring were heard through the night.

The following morning we woke nice and early as the bright sunlight shone through the thin curtains. Ace and I went for a run with John. The grass was very wet with dew. After breakfast Lyn and Kath packed a few things into a bag and we were soon off down the track to the beach, which was completely deserted. There was no change in the sea since last night. The kids were soon in the water, and Ace and I followed; it was great fun swimming through the waves. Marc picked me up and Phil took Ace. They carried us out into deeper water beyond the waves - here we could swim with the boys, which was great fun. Faith and Gina joined us. I got picked up by a large wave and was carried in on the crest, only to be unceremoniously dumped on the beach. I was told by Marc that this was 'surfing' and I thoroughly enjoyed it. Soon afterwards Ace came in the same way. We shook ourselves and went off to investigate some rocks at one end of the beach. There were some strange creatures in amongst the rocks. They had long front arms with claws on the end and I soon learnt that they could give a painful nip. Eventually I heard Master calling and we returned to where everyone was sitting. We were given a bowl of water and some dog biscuits; swimming had made us hungry. After this we slept on the sand in the sun, which was quite hot.

Later in the day everybody went for a swim and of course Ace and I were not going to be left out. The water was beautifully cool after lying in the hot sun. The boys took us out beyond the waves again but I wanted to surf and came in on a lovely wave. After landing on the beach I barked and Phil came and fetched me and carried me out again. In I zoomed again but this time Ace came in as well. I barked again and Marc and Phil collected us. This was great fun and we continued for quite a while; my ears were full of water.

After some time we returned to the caravan and a meal was cooked, which was eaten on chairs and tables outside the caravan, there were no pickings for us. Much later we took everyone for an evening walk along the path, passing the beach, and on along the cliff. The air was full of scents. In one field we had our leads put on as there were sheep grazing - they are the strangest creatures. As we walked back along the cliff it was beginning to get dark. There was a moon rising in the sky above the bay, its reflection glistened and shimmered in the gentle water below us. We all slept well that night!

The next few days were spent on the beach and it was really hot. Ace and I became very good at surfing. Another game that Phil and Marc played with us was a game of ball, where they would throw it to each other and we had to catch it. One night after a particularly hot, muggy day we all went to bed fairly early. Ace had got into the routine of sleeping in my bed. Rain started to fall, it sounded really heavy and loud on the roof of the caravan. Suddenly there was a bright flash which was followed almost immediately by a tremendous clap of thunder that woke everyone up. Ace and I stayed low in our bed; I for one did not like thunder. Master and John got up and we settled down in their laps as the storm raged outside. The rain on the roof was deafening.

The storm eventually moved away but the rain continued until daylight the following morning when we all got up. Ace and I took Lyn and Kath for a walk around the field; the air was cool and fresh. The grass was very wet and the sheep looked bedraggled. The next few days were spent visiting places and Ace and I spent a lot of time guarding the cars. Every morning and evening we took Master and John for a walk down to the beach. The sea was rough and the waves were huge (well I thought they were anyway). We went up onto the rocks at one end where the creatures with long arms and huge claws on the end were.

As the weather improved we were back on the beach. One evening Master and John cooked a meal outside the caravan on a strange contraption. There was a lot of smoke coming from it and delicious scents. While I sat on Marc's lap watching intently he told me that it was a 'Bar B Q'. The meat that came off it was delicious (we got some tiny morsels). Master and John were drinking out of big glasses;

I believe the drink was beer as I had heard the word a lot during the holiday!

The following day turned out to be our last day there. After breakfast we all went for a long walk in the opposite direction to the beach. There were a lot of rabbit holes to examine. We also found one that had bedding outside. I was about to investigate but Master grabbed me and John picked up Ace. Master told me that it was a 'no, no' as it was a 'badger sett' whatever that was. The rest of the day was spent on the beach. The sea was a lot calmer so Ace and I had a good swim. Gina and Faith were building curious shapes out of sand, some looked like houses of a sort. Back at the caravan John and Master loaded up the cars with all the cases and my bed and, after a few sandwiches and a drink, we all got into the cars. As the light started to go we drove out of the field. Ace was with me on the back shelf where we slept heavily.

We stopped twice and on the second occasion after a quick stretch of the legs and a toilet Ace went into the other car. I then slept on Phil's lap which was nice and warm. He and Gina were sound asleep. After what seemed an age we turned into the back yard of the police house. There was no sign of Ace or John and Kath.

So ended a lovely holiday in North Wales.

Fire!

Life soon returned to normal after the holiday, but I did miss Ace. It was the time that Master had once described to me as the 'harvest', when the crops were gathered in. All I knew about the harvest was that once the fields were cleared it gave me a lot more space!

One morning Master and I were out in the police car. It had been a quiet morning and Master had called at a few houses with papers in his hands whilst I guarded the car. That was about to change when Master spoke on the radio and we were off with the deafening sound of the siren. We sped through Thaxted and along some country lanes. Out of the back window I saw a fire engine close behind us with all its lights flashing, its siren was even louder than ours. Master pulled over and let it pass and we then followed it. I suddenly saw a lot of smoke coming out of a field and the fire engine pulled over and stopped. We drove past and I became aware that there were two more fire engines ahead with firemen already in the field. I could see the flames roaring through the crop, the strong wind fanning the flames, there was smoke everywhere. Way ahead of the fire engines Master stopped the car and got out with his helmet on; I watched out of the back window. The dense smoke was sweeping across the lane and through the haze a car appeared ahead of us. Master stopped it and spoke to the driver who turned the car around and drove off.

When I looked back the sight was quite spectacular. The flames had reached the hedge and within seconds the hedge was reduced to a black, smouldering skeleton. The flames had leapt the lane and the bank on the other side was alight.

Despite the efforts of the two firemen the flames were soon racing through the crop in the next field. The flames were unrelenting as they sped through this field, the breadth of the flames getting wider and wider. A fire engine appeared through the smoke and drove past us, soon followed by another. Master got back into the car and we followed them. Master tried to explain to me that they were trying to 'head off' the fire. I didn't understand what he meant but I knew that it was exciting. We followed the engines for some distance until we stopped again. I could see clearly over the field where the fire was racing across. A tractor was in the field and firemen were racing around with huge pipes that Master described as 'hoses'. Smoke was billowing across the field ahead of the flames which stretched right across the field. Master was out of the car but the increasing wind was fanning the flames and he soon had to get back in and move the car out of danger. The tractor driver was trying to clear some of the crop to create what Master described as a 'fire break'. Suddenly all the firemen in the field came rushing out and leapt into their engines. They were on the move as the wall of flames swept towards them. The tractor was behind the hedge and was speeding towards the entrance where the firemen had come from, but the driver had left it too late and, at the last minute, he leapt from the tractor, ran for the gateway and into the lane. Master ran along the lane to the man and grabbed him. He rushed him back to the police car; the man was coughing violently. He sat in the front of the car as we moved off. Master spoke on the radio and I looked out of the back window. The flames had engulfed the tractor and the hedge beyond - the tractor was well alight. Two firemen tried to get in close but were beaten back as the entire hedge line caught fire. Black smoke was billowing from the tractor and shortly afterwards there were two loud explosions from it and the black smoke intensified.

It was not long before an ambulance pulled up in front of us and Master helped the man, who was still coughing, into the ambulance. The main front of the fire had leapt the road and was consuming another field at a tremendous rate. With the main fire now gone the firemen had been able to get into the field and were pouring a strange white substance onto the now charred remains of the tractor. The flames were soon out. The hedge was still smouldering and sparks were flying out of it on the wind. The ambulance left and two fire engines passed us; we followed them. They parked up a short distance further on and we went on for a few minutes before pulling off the road into a field of stubble. I could see the flames just entering the field along the bottom. We were fairly high up overlooking a valley across a field of stubble. On the far side of the field was another tractor moving up and down as fast as it could go with a huge set of metal discs on the back. As we watched, a second police car pulled up alongside ours and we all got out. Smoke was billowing across the field ahead of us with the flames sweeping across the stubble. Master was talking to his colleague and I was sitting upright to get a better view. I suddenly saw a fox running ahead of the flames. It streaked across the field, passed in front of the tractor and disappeared through the hedge. It was almost immediately followed by a hare that shot across the field below us and through the hedge.

The fire had reached the area where the tractor had been working and the work that the tractor had done stopped the flames advancing. Almost immediately I saw a strange thing in the middle of the field ahead of us. The wind was whipping up the ash in the field creating a tube that was spinning up high into the sky. More and more ash got swept up into the tube as it swept across the field, and it went higher and higher into the sky. It reached the hedge and passed through it. At this point the funnel appeared to lose its speed and it slowly broke up with ash raining down in the wind. Master stood talking for a while. With the major fire front now stopped, the firemen soon had the other fires under control. We eventually left the field and drove around for quite a while checking that there were no more fires. We stopped several times to speak to policemen and firemen before returning to the police house as the sun was setting. It had been an exciting day and you can guess what I dreamt about that night!

The Rat and the Fox

One morning Kath, John, the kids and Ace arrived early. After they had drunk a quick cup of tea we all drove up to the other end of Thaxted to an area known as the 'tennis courts' where Master, Lyn, John and Kath did something quite strange. They started knocking a ball to each other over a net with a strange contraption in their hands. They ran around all over the place, chasing the ball. Ace and I stayed with the kids on the bench outside the court; we were on our leads. They were getting very hot chasing this ball around, I was getting hot just watching them! I have come to the conclusion that humans do some strange things. Eventually they came out of the court with sweat pouring off them, laughing. We returned to the house where they sat out in the garden at a table eating and drinking, it was a really hot sunny day.

Afterwards Master and John put our leads on and led us out of the gate. The kids were playing in the garden. I led Master, John and Ace down to the river where it was very shallow, except for one spot on a sharp bend in the river where the water was always deep. Ace and I climbed down the steep bank at this point and jumped in. It was lovely and cool and we swam around. Master and John watched us for a while and then walked on. I got worried when they disappeared out of sight so I ran up the bank until I could see them. I ran flat out with Ace behind me and caught them up at the crossroads in the footpath where one path leads to the windmill (a curious round building with strange outstretched arms) and the other path leads to Cutlers Green. I assumed that we were going to head towards the windmill as we usually did, but on this occasion we turned towards Cutlers Green.

The path led us through a field with crops on both sides, which I learnt was wheat. I hadn't been along here for some time. This was the path that Master took if Dave was with us on a long walk. We walked through to the green and eventually to the old railway track beyond. Ace and I were busy investigating any interesting scents and there were plenty of them while Master and John were deep in conversation. The old railway line was a really interesting place - it was very overgrown.

As soon as we started to walk along this track, Ace disturbed a rat which darted down into a ditch that ran alongside the track. This was as far as it got for, like a flash, Ace was on it and with a quick flick of his head the rat was dead. We both sniffed it as Master and John came over to look at it. Ace picked up the limp body, its head hung out one side of his mouth and the long tail out of the other. He was about to walk off with his prize but John had other ideas. He picked Ace up, still holding firmly onto the rat, and managed to open Ace's jaw with finger pressure on the side of his mouth. The rat was released. Ace was not happy but as we walked off he soon forgot about it. I never saw what happened to the rat.

We walked off along the track in amongst all the undergrowth. Suddenly Ace and I picked up a very strong scent; we followed it, full of excitement. As we raced ahead of the two men the scent was getting stronger. Then we saw ahead of us a huge dog fox running through the undergrowth away from us. We gave chase - this was really exciting - so much so that we both started barking. The fox was a magnificent animal with a deep red colour and a white tip to his tail. We had soon left the men way back and were still at full pelt, when the dense undergrowth would allow.

The fox suddenly turned off the track, cleared the ditch in one leap and disappeared into the tall brown wheat but he was not going to get away that easily. Ace gave out a loud bark as we jumped over the ditch and ran into the wheat; the scent was really strong on the stems of the wheat where the fox had just passed. Way off in the distance I heard Master and John calling our names but we ignored them, this was much more fun. Ace was slightly faster than me and was ahead, crashing through the wheat; I was following in his wake. We ran on and on but the fox was getting away.

After crossing two more fields I think we realised that we were not going to catch this animal so we slowed to a stop and stood panting heavily. I could faintly hear the men's voices calling way off in the distance. It took us quite a while to return to the railway track and to Master and John who were both very pleased to see us.

The rest of the walk was fairly uneventful and we eventually arrived home. After all the excitement and the heat we were both exhausted. We had a good drink and stretched out on the lawn. Much later, John, Kath, the kids and Ace left. It seemed very quiet after they had gone. I missed Ace, he was great fun but I slept well that night dreaming of giant rats and foxes!

Soon after the fun with Ace a strange feeling came over me. I was very restless and I had a really strong urge to find a mate. Master explained to me that I was 'on heat' whatever that meant. I was confined to the garden for most of the time and when I did go for a walk I was not allowed off the lead, even to see Dave and Grace. I did not like it at all, was my life changing forever? Fortunately this strange feeling did not last long and soon life was back to normal.

The Cottage

The next few weeks were fairly uneventful. We went on regular walks with the kids to school, including my biscuits with Dave and Grace, and walks around the fields near the house. But one day an event occurred that was to change our lives. We had got up early and after breakfast we all got into the car and drove off. We travelled for quite a while; I slept on the back shelf.

I woke with a start when the car stopped and the doors opened. My lead was put on and Lyn led me out of the car. We had stopped outside a little cottage which was next door to a tiny little village shop. I was told that we were in a village called Wighton, near Wells-Next-The-Sea - all I knew was that there were a lot of interesting scents worth investigating.

We went into the cottage which was cold and empty. There were carpets down with some very exciting smells on but there was little else. I went off and investigated once Lyn had slipped my lead. I scampered up the stairs and was surprised to find there was no furniture in any of the rooms.

I was called back downstairs and we all went out into the garden - I followed Gina and Phil. The garden was interesting as we had to climb up some steps to get onto the small lawn and I was at eye level with the kitchen window. I 'christened' the lawn while everyone else walked around the small garden talking. I could smell the sea and knew that it couldn't be far away then we went back through the cottage and out to the car.

We drove the short distance to Wells, where we walked along the quay. There was a lot of water there and some strange birds floating on the surface. They were all shapes and sizes but there were some really huge ones which were all white. I later learnt that these were 'swans', and could be dangerous! We walked alongside the water for quite a long way. Lyn and Master were deep in conversation, and not really taking a lot of notice of what I or Phil and Gina were doing. I was rummaging through the rocks just above the water line, while Phil and Gina were throwing stones in to the water, missing the birds of course!

Eventually as the sun set and the evening got darker we went back to the car and returned to the cottage. We did not go in but sat outside in the car. I, of course, had grabbed my favourite place on the back shelf. Lyn and Master sat talking for a long time before we set off for home.

A few weeks later we returned to the cottage in a huge van while Phil and Gina were at school. I had ridden up on Lyn's lap as there was no rear shelf, Master was driving. The back of the van was full of furniture, which Lyn and Master unloaded into the cottage. I had to watch from the side window of the front seat. There were even a few bags of logs unloaded but I could not understand what they were for. We then drove into the village and I was left in the van whilst Lyn and Master went into the pub. They later came back to the van smelling strongly of fish and chips. I was very disgruntled and slept in Lyn's lap all the way home in a huff!

Shortly after this visit Master and I returned to the cottage in the van but this time it was with several bags of logs, which were stored in an area in the back garden. I was soon to learn what they were for.

The Prisoner

One evening Master and I were out in the police car. It was dark and very windy outside. We had been patrolling the lanes all around Thaxted for quite a while and it had been a quiet evening but that was all set to change after Master spoke on the police radio.

The roof flights were set to flash and I could see them flashing against a nearby hedge. As the car sped off I squeezed between the front seats and jumped up onto the back shelf as this was the safest place to be when Master was in a hurry.

We raced around the back roads for quite a while; my claws held me firm as they dug deep into the shelf material. We came around a corner with tall, bare trees on either side and there in the middle of the road was a car on its roof. Master stopped the car and leapt out leaving me to guard the car. I jumped down from the shelf and sat upright on the front seat to watch what was happening.

I saw Master on his hands and knees reaching into the car, he was trying to get the driver out but appeared to be having some difficulty. Eventually Master pulled the man from the car, as the rain started falling heavily. The man appeared to be very unsteady on his feet and was swaying as Master walked him over to the police car and placed him in the back seat. I stayed where I was. There was a strong smell coming from the man which I recognised from occasions at home when Master had drunk beer. Master got in, reached over to a pocket in front of me and took out a black box. I watched him as he assembled the box and then turned and spoke to the man, who up till this point had been quiet.

However, as Master spoke to him he started shouting. He tried to open the door of the car but he couldn't. Master held the black box out towards the man but he lashed out hard and the box flew out of Master's hand, narrowly missing me. I was rapidly taking a dislike to this man. Master spoke to him again and he appeared to calm down. At this point a second police car arrived and Master spoke briefly to the two officers. We then went, leaving them at the scene.

We had only gone a short distance when the man started shouting again and once again tried to open the door. Suddenly he grabbed Master around the throat with both hands. Master stopped the car abruptly, in fact so suddenly that I ended up on the floor. By the time I got back up onto the seat, Master had freed himself from the man and had placed his handcuffs on him. He then spoke briefly on the radio, as the man took a swing at Master with his handcuffed hands. I bared my teeth and was about to lunge at him but Master told me very firmly to "stay", so I did. Master reached over and took a firm hold of the handcuffs. The man was still shouting and thrashing around in the seat. Shortly another police car arrived and a big policeman got into the back of our car and took hold of the handcuffs on the man. Master then drove off with the other police car following along behind us.

The man continued shouting and struggling in the back of the car but he was held firmly by the huge policemen who virtually filled the back seat. I recognised his scent, he had been in the office before and had made a fuss of me; I liked him!

Eventually we arrived at Saffron Walden Police Station and Master and the big PC walked the man inside while I kept guard in the police car. Master was gone for some time. I feel asleep to the sound of the rain on the roof.

Master woke me with a bit of a start as he got back into the car and we drove off. Master explained to me that the man had been a 'drink driver' and of course as usual I fully understood what he meant! We returned home and I dreamt of fights in the back of the police car, which of course I won.

The Show

Being fairly small, if ever I got muddy I would be unceremoniously dunked in a sink and washed. Although I loved water I did not like this. One evening I was given a fairly thorough bath in the kitchen sink. I couldn't really understand why as I was not particularly dirty. I had the full works including a shampoo, which Master was very careful not to get in my eyes. Lyn dried me off in a towel (I enjoyed that) and I had a thorough brush. I smelt awful, well I thought I did, so at the first opportunity I had a good roll on my blanket in my basket; the only trouble was that Lyn had washed that as well!

The following morning I still smelt awful. Everyone was up early and straight out after breakfast. Following a very quick walk around the recreation ground we were all in the car and off out somewhere. I sat up on the back shelf and was soon asleep. We had a long journey but eventually arrived in a field where there were a lot of cars parked. The air was rich with the scent of other dogs and I got really excited. Phil and Gina got out and I followed. There were dogs everywhere and they were all Jack Russell Terriers like me. I wanted to go off and investigate and 'introduce' myself to some of them but Lyn in a flash had placed my lead on; I was quite disappointed. Some dogs were on leads, some in cages being carried, and others in baskets. They all appeared to be heading in the same direction and we followed. We entered another field where there were large canvas constructions and areas roped off. We stopped near one of the roped-off areas and we sat down on a large blanket that Lyn had spread out.

I stretched on my lead and introduced myself to a little Jack Russell that was sitting behind us. She was smaller and younger than me, and quite nice. We spent quite a lot of time sniffing each other. She smelt quite nice, not like me! Another terrier and his Master came and sat next to us; we greeted each other. He was really handsome and smelt good. The little bitch behind me joined in and we all sniffed each other. There were terriers everywhere - I had never seen so many - this was wonderful. A fight broke out on the other side of the roped off area between two terriers, but the Masters soon broke it up. Fights were starting everywhere as more and more terriers arrived at this roped off area. The air was full of the sound of barking and arguing terriers.

Lyn brought out a huge amount of food from a large plastic box that Master had carried from the car. Everybody sat and ate sandwiches and biscuits; I was given a few tit bits. Master called this a 'picnic', it was certainly noisy. I was given a bowl of water - it was hot and sunny and I was thirsty. We sat there for quite a while and the fights continued. Eventually Master stood up and led me away. I passed a lot of terriers and eventually we entered the roped-off area which Master told me was the 'ring', following a number of terriers on leads with their Masters. In the middle of the ring there stood a very important-looking woman. She was watching us all. We all stood in a line facing her. Master told me that she was the 'judge' and I must 'be nice to her and behave' - as if I wouldn't!

We walked around in a big circle with the judge in the middle. Master was pulling up on my lead to keep my head up but I wanted to investigate all the scents being left by the other dogs.

We stopped quite suddenly and I watched as a table was brought into the area. The first terrier in the line was picked up by its Master and placed on the table. The judge then gave the animal a very close examination, handling it all over whilst its Master held her head quite firmly. I saw it bare its fine set of teeth on at least two occasions. The next one was placed on the table and just as the judge was about to start her examination, the terrier leapt off and disappeared under the rope before vanishing into the crowd, pursued by its very anxious Master. Almost at the same time a fight broke out between two dogs ahead of me. They were fighting tooth and nail and both drew blood from each other. Several dogs on the other side of the rope got very excited and wanted to join in. Eventually the respective Masters managed to separate the blood-covered dogs which were carried out, quite unceremoniously, from the ring. The next up onto the table was a very handsome dog who sat perfectly while the judge prodded and nudged him. There were another two ahead of me, then it was my turn. Master picked me up and gently put me on the table, he kept on saying to me "Be a good girl". It felt like being at the vets, and I didn't like that. I was distracted by another fight that broke out between two bitches behind the rope but they were rapidly separated. With my examination over, Master lifted me back down on to the ground and praised me, which I liked. After the last dog was examined (a very small, dark terrier dog called Rambo) we all walked around the judge again until she asked us to stop. Rambo was right behind me, he was a really handsome dog and I introduced myself to him while Master spoke to his Master.

We stood there for quite a while sniffing at each other while the judge walked along the line both front and back. Rambo and I were getting bored with this, we wanted to go off and explore. Lyn and the others were watching us from the sidelines. I pulled hard on my lead but Master held me fast. Suddenly Rambo's name was called out by the judge and he led his Master forward to her. After a shake of hands, his Master was given a rosette and a certificate. Everybody around the ring clapped and cheered as Rambo and his smiling Master returned to the line next to me, he was a popular dog.

We greeted each other while the two Masters shook hands. Rambo and I were preoccupied and I suddenly heard the judge call out my name. Master stepped forward and I followed, I would have preferred to stay with Rambo but I was not given the choice. Master shook hands with the judge, who then reached down and patted me on the head and said “Well done”. Master was given a rosette and a certificate and we returned to the line. Everybody was clapping, Lyn was smiling, and Phil and Gina were cheering loudly. A third dog was called out of the line, a young bitch called Kip and the last rosette and certificate was handed out to her. After more applause we all walked out of the ring. We returned to Lyn and the others and they examined the rosette and certificate, they were really excited, although I didn't see what all the fuss was about.

After finishing the picnic we went for a walk around the grounds; there were terriers everywhere! One big bruiser of a dog tried to bite me as we passed but I was not having that and retaliated by nipping him hard on his muzzle. A fight almost broke out but Master pulled me back, I was disappointed, but I taught him not to mess with me! On the other side of the field there were some games and races going on involving the terriers and their Masters - these looked like fun. One of the games involved a terrier being placed in a very long twisting and turning plastic tunnel and the dog was timed on how long it would take to travel to the other end. Master knew that I loved tunnels and when my turn came I was placed in the tunnel. There were some tremendous scents in the tunnel, including one I recognised as Rambo's. I ran along the tunnel, it was quite dark but great fun. I could hear Master calling from the other end, his voice getting louder as I ran along. But I suddenly stopped as there was a strong and interesting scent on the floor of the tunnel. I smelt it hard before moving on. Eventually I could see daylight ahead and Master's head in the tunnel. I ran up to him and he was on his knees. I jumped up into his arms with such force that I sent him flying! Lyn and the others were nearby laughing. While I had him on the ground I licked his face and beard, he was laughing so much he couldn't get up. Needless to say I didn't win the prize.

Another game was also very interesting - it was an assault course. A group of terriers were lined up and on a shout of "Go" they ran up a plank, down the other side, through a short tunnel, through some hoops and finally under a huge tarpaulin. We watched as the terriers got totally confused and after they all went under the tarpaulin a huge fight broke out in the middle. Loads of people crawled under the cover to retrieve their dogs and this looked like good fun. I was in the next bunch of terriers to go through. I was tugging on my lead to go when suddenly we were off. Master ran alongside me as I cleared the planks and the tunnel, and then went through the hoops - this was great fun. We all seemed to reach the tarpaulin at the same time and under we went. It was dark and hot under there and I crawled through fairly quickly. As I crawled towards the other side I could see daylight approaching. Suddenly there was a commotion behind me - a fight had broken out. I was about to turn around and join in but a huge hand reached in under the cover and grabbed the scruff of my neck. The next moment I was out in the bright sunlight sitting next to Master. The fight under the tarpaulin was in full swing with various Masters clambering under the cover to retrieve their dogs. I wanted to go again and join the fun but my lead was put back on and off we went.

We found a large area where there were tables and chairs and people were sitting drinking tea. We sat at a table, and I spotted Rambo under the next table. I managed to stretch on my lead to get closer to him, Master saw me and gave me some slack. We greeted each other and I lay down next to him. It was really hot, and Lyn brought us over a bowl of water, which between us we emptied. A fight broke out under a nearby table and we both watched as the two fighting terriers got really stuck in. Empty chairs went flying until their respective Masters managed to separate them - not an easy task! We eventually walked away from the table. I said goodbye to Rambo, who watched me walk away and though I kept turning around to see him, he was soon out of sight.

Before long we were back at the car in the field, along with a lot of other terriers, as the show was coming to an end. We joined the queue to get out which took quite a while. As I watched out of the back window I suddenly spotted Rambo looking out of the window of a car alongside us. I barked excitedly and was promptly told to be quiet. If only I could get out. Even jumping down from the rear shelf onto Phil's lap, didn't help. I squeezed between the two front seats and sat on Lyn's lap watching out of the windscreen as Rambo's car disappeared. He was watching out of the rear window and our eyes met for one last time as his car turned out of the field. I was never to see him again which was a great shame as I really fancied him!

We had a long drive home but I couldn't settle down. Eventually I fell into a deep sleep that night after such an exciting day. Inevitably I dreamt about Rambo and all the other terriers at the show.

A Cooked Breakfast

One morning, we were all bundled into the car and I watched from the back shelf as suitcases were placed in the boot. We soon set off and I was asleep almost immediately waking to the familiar scents of the sea and fields. We were at Wighton and the cottage. It was cold outside as well as inside the cottage but Master soon had a roaring fire warming us all up. Later in the day there was a knock at the door and I barked. Lyn went to the door and there were Martin and Andrea standing with their suitcases. I knew them as we had visited them on a number of occasions, and they had frequently stayed at the police house. We greeted each other. Later in the evening we all disappeared down to the pub where the humans had a meal. I sat under the table waiting for any scraps but none were forthcoming so I curled up in front of the huge fire nearby. It was late when we got back to the cottage and the wind was really cold. Phil slept downstairs and I curled up with him.

The following morning I went out onto the back lawn as Master collected a pile of logs. There was a light dusting of snow on the grass. When I came back in everybody had come down and were sitting around in the front room. Martin was sitting in front of the fire with a small shovel in his hand, which he was holding in the flames. There was a strange sizzling sound coming from the fire and a delicious smell wafting through the room. Plates were brought in, and one by one they were filled with food. Martin gave me a piece of bacon which I thoroughly enjoyed, I did like Martin! Everybody sat around eating their food. Phil gave me a bacon rind and I had the scrapings off the other plates when everyone had finished. Lyn placed them in my bowl and Martin placed an egg on top. I really enjoyed this cooked breakfast and for the next few days this was the order of the day. I always looked forward to breakfast!

The Swan

Early one morning we drove over to see John and Kath. Ace and I greeted each other like old friends. We played in the back garden for a while chasing around on the small lawn, which was great fun as always. Eventually John and Master came out and I heard the magic word 'walkies'. Our leads were put on and we were soon out of the back gate walking briskly down to a beautiful area that Master called the 'lakes'. Ace and I were quickly in the cool water swimming around. John and Master were walking along the bank, talking.

As we swam out towards a small island I spotted a pair of huge white birds on the edge of the island. One was sitting on a large bed of reeds and vegetation, the other was standing nearby. As we approached, the one that was standing moved down off the island into the water, and it was then that I realised just how big this bird was, and that he was swimming towards us in a threatening manner! Ace started to swim off in the opposite direction, back to the bank where John and Master were calling us. In my wisdom I decided to confront this bird and just let him know who was boss. We drew closer and closer to each other. Its wings went up on its back which made the bird look even bigger. Master was now really shouting loudly now but still I ignored him.

Suddenly, the bird lunged at me, taking me a little by surprise. It hit with its wing so hard that I sank momentarily. I resurfaced amidst a load of bubbles and the bird was still there, pounding the water with its wing but fortunately missing me. I swam away towards the bank where Master and John were shouting at me. Ace was up on the bank as well, standing next to John and looking intently at me.

The bird, however, had other ideas and swam after me. It hit me again really hard on the head, its wing pushing me under water for a second time. As I came up Master threw something at the swan that landed in the water right next to the bird and startled it. In the confusion I made my escape towards the bank which was fairly close now. But the bird had not quite finished with me yet. It lunged at me so hard with its wing that it struck me on the head and pushed me deep under water. The next thing I knew was a hand grabbed me by the scruff of the neck and I was lifted briskly out of the water, high into the sky. I was held firmly in Master's grip and I could see the bird swimming back to the island. I struggled to break Master's grip as I wanted to have another go at the bird that was swimming away victoriously, but Master would not let me go. As we walked off Master held me firmly - by the tone of his voice he was not happy. The bottom half of his shirt and his trousers were soaked and John was laughing at us. The swan returned to its mate on the island with its head held high and watched us as we moved away.

I remained wound up for the rest of the day; I think that Ace sensed this and kept his distance. I slept on Gina's lap all the way home dreaming of giant white birds!

The Owl

One evening I was sitting on Master's feet in the office, as he sat at his desk working on some papers which I heard being shuffled. Suddenly there was a knock at the door. I barked and ran towards it. Outside there was a man carrying a cardboard box.

As he spoke to Master I heard a shuffling sound coming from the box that had been placed on the counter. I got very curious but was too short to investigate. After speaking to the man, Master put on a pair of gloves and carefully opened the box. He reached inside and a loud shuffle was heard. Out came a big bird in Master's hand. It was a curious bird, with a huge head and forward-facing eyes. I stood up on my back legs to sniff it and the bird glared down at me and hissed. I jumped back and barked loudly. Master looked at the bird before placing it back in the box. The man then left the office leaving the box on the counter. After he left Master took the bird out of the box again and sat on his chair to examine it closely. I sat and watched as he turned it this way and that. The bird's eyes were fixed on me the whole time. It was eventually placed back in the box and the top was sealed. Master told me that it was a 'tawny owl'.

The following morning Master went to the office early and I ran between his legs as we entered the office. The owl was out of the box and was sitting on the high back of Master's seat at his desk. As we appeared it flew off the seat and ended up over the other side of the counter. I went to chase it but the counter door was closed. Master went through and closed the door behind him; the next thing I saw was the owl in Master's gloved hands. He placed it back in the box and put a book on top.

As darkness fell Master returned to the office, picked up the box and left via the outside door, I followed. We got into the car and drove off, I sat on the front passenger seat - the box was on the rear seat. We drove for a short distance in the dark and parked up in a field gateway near a wood. Master got out and collected the box whilst I was left in the car. Master carried the box to the front of the car and in the headlights I watched as he opened the box and then stood back. Almost immediately the owl rose out of the box, flew over Master's head and into the trees, out of sight. We watched for a while before returning home.

The Kestrel

Not long after the owl had been returned to the wild another bird arrived in a box in the office. Again with gloved hands Master took the bird from the box. It was another curious-looking bird and was also very noisy. It glared at me as Master checked it over. Master told me that this was a 'kestrel'. This time the bird was placed back in its box and carried out into the shed in the back garden, where it remained for a couple of days. Master then brought in a cage of wood and wire, which was placed on the lawn. A small log was placed in the cage and the bird was then put into it. I watched with fascination as the kestrel sat on the log in the cage and glared at me. It had one wing hanging down. I went to move closer but Master spoke sternly to me so I sat down and just looked on. A dead mouse was put in the cage and the bird grabbed it and tore it to bits on the log. I lay down on the grass and watched. That night the bird was back in its box and in the shed only to return to the aviary the following day. This was the pattern for the next few days - by night the bird was in the shed and during the day it returned to the aviary where it was given food. Master and Lyn ensured that I could not get too close to the bird.

As the days and weeks went by the kestrel became stronger and its wing appeared to mend as the bird started to fly around the aviary. One morning Master brought the box out of the shed and carried it around to the waste ground behind the house, I followed excitedly with Lyn who picked me up as Master put the box down. He then carefully opened the box and stood back. The kestrel flew out of the box and landed in a nearby tree. We stood and watched it as it took off again and flew high into the clear sky before eventually disappearing over the trees.

Over the years to come I was to get used to all manner of creatures arriving at the office.

A 'Monster' in the Sky

It was a hot sunny day and Master and Dave were on duty in the police car, with me sitting up on the back shelf. We were parked in a field gateway and were watching cars go by on the road in front of us. Dave was so big that I couldn't see much on his side so I was watching proceedings over Master's shoulder. Master and Dave were talking when Master suddenly reached down and picked up the police radio and spoke into it. Shortly afterwards we were on the road and there was a lovely cool breeze coming in through the open windows, along with some interesting scents.

We travelled for quite a while before turning into a large farmyard. Master and Dave got out and I was told to "stay". I did as I was told but I managed to squeeze though to the front seat and hang out of the open window to watch. Master spoke to a man who I recognised; he had called in at the office on a number of occasions. Master came over and let me out and we all walked through the yard, past some huge barns and out into a field beyond. On the other side of this field there was a small wood which we walked through; there were some strong rabbit scents.

The sight that greeted us on the other side frightened me and I kept in close to Master's feet. There ahead of us was a huge, long 'monster' with wings on one end, floating high above us on a long line that was tied to the back of a huge tractor. Master, Dave and the man laughed as they approached it. I started barking and ran off; I didn't like it at all. Master called me back but I ran on to the safety of the wood. I stopped, turned around and looked at the monster with dread. It was still moving around, high in the blue sky, and I still did not like it. I was worried for Master and Dave who were both standing underneath the monster. I crept out from the safety of the trees and slowly moved towards Master. Suddenly in a gust of wind the monster dived out of the sky towards me. I barked at it and ran back to the trees.

Dave and Master started pulling on the thick cord holding the monster and it slowly started dropping out of the sky but it was still swinging wildly in the breeze. Down and down it came until it was only a few feet above the tractor. As I watched, the man got into the tractor and started the engine. The tractor then started moving very slowly and Master and Dave walked along behind the monster. I was not going to be left behind so I ran over to Master and trotted along behind him. We went along a track around the outside of the wood and eventually arrived in the yard where the police car was parked.

There then followed a long discussion between Master, Dave and the man. They were examining the monster, far too closely for my liking, and I stood well back with my hackles up ready to pounce if it decided to attack anyone. It was swaying in the wind despite Dave holding on to its 'lead'. Eventually Master and Dave folded all the aerials down on the roof of the police car and the monster was taken off the tractor and tied down onto the roof of the car. Although still nervous of it I felt a lot better once it was secured. The tail of the monster was hanging over the back of the car, almost touching the ground. The head of it was slightly hanging over the front.

A short while later we were in the car driving very slowly out of the farm yard. As I looked very apprehensively out of the back of the car from the back shelf, Master laughed and said "It is only a barrage balloon Cassie, it's alright". Whatever it was I did not like it! We drove down narrow country lanes very, very slowly, but eventually we arrived back in Thaxted and the police house rear yard. I jumped out of the car and hid behind Lyn who had come out to watch as Dave and Master released the monster. The wind was blowing quite hard, and the two men were having difficulty holding onto it as it thrashed around in the sky above us.

Eventually it was forced into the garage, it only just fitted and as the door was slammed shut I was quite relieved. I wasn't at all happy about it being in the garage and for the next few days I continually sniffed under the garage door, I could smell it. Eventually a huge lorry reversed up the drive and I watched as the balloon was loaded on board. I was really glad to see it leave.

Goats

Early one morning I had taken Master for a walk across the recreation field and we ended up in the rear garden of The Fox and Hounds Public House where Master stood and talked to a man in uniform. It was not a police uniform - Master later told me that he was an 'RSPCA Inspector', which obviously meant nothing to me. They walked over to where two curious animals were eating grass. They were the strangest animals I had ever seen and I started barking at them. They could not run off as they were held firm on chains pegged into the ground. One was white and the other was multi coloured. Master told me to be quiet but, as usual, I did as I was told and I kept barking! Master shouted at me and I got the message.

Soon afterwards Master pulled out one of the pegs attached to the chain and the other man pulled out the other. The goats were lead out of the garden. I kept behind Master, I did not like goats. We walked across the recreation ground and out of the entrance which was almost opposite the police house. We went across the road and the goats were pulling really hard; Master was having a job holding onto his and to me. As we went around the back of the house onto the waste ground Lyn joined us and took my lead. The goats' pegs were knocked into the ground and they started eating the long grass.

Later the same day a small van with no wheels was dumped around the back and as the sun set, the goats were lead into the van in which Master had placed a thick layer of straw on the floor. The doors were shut.

The following morning I went around the back with Lyn and Master, and the goats were let out. They had their collars fixed to the chains and Master then knocked the pegs into the ground. I moved in to get a better look at these strange animals but as I got closer to one of them, it dropped its head and charged at me. I ran off barking, as Lyn and Master laughed out loud. I decided again that I definitely did not like goats!

A few days later Master and I were in the office. Master was sitting at his desk and I was lying by the office door. Suddenly I heard a sound outside and looked out. There were the two goats walking past the door, dragging their chains behind them. They walked down the drive towards the road. I barked loudly but Master told me to be quiet. I barked again and jumped up at the glass, the goats had reached the road. Master looked up and out and immediately ran to the door and rushed out. I tried to follow but Master told me very firmly to "stay" and closed the door. I watched him run off down the road in pursuit of the goats that were running flat out away from him. Lyn came out of the house door and joined in the chase then they all disappeared out of sight. I ran through to the house to see if I could get a better view but I couldn't see anything, so I went back to the office door. I soon saw Master and Lyn each dragging back a very reluctant goat. They walked along the drive and disappeared around the back.

A few months later a further incident occurred with the goats which rather angered Master. On the waste ground, near to the entrance of the back yard, Master had dug some ground over and planted a load of plants which were growing well, I believe he had called them 'cabbages, broccoli and cauliflower'. One morning I had gone around the back with Master as usual to let the goats out and peg them out on a new patch of grass. This done we returned to the house and as we passed the plants Master stopped and looked at them. They were now much taller than me.

Later the same day I was resting out in the garden with Master and Lyn. Suddenly I heard a sound that made me run to the back gate: it was the goat's chain. I barked loudly but was told to be quiet. I barked again and jumped at the gate causing Master to come over and open it. I ran out barking and Master ran after me, for he had seen what I had seen. The goats were happily devouring the plants that Master had grown. He shouted at them so loudly that I stopped running and sat quietly as Master waded through the plants and grabbed both the chains. He led the goats out of the plants and they were unceremoniously returned to the van. By the tone of Master's voice I gathered that he was not at all happy as he inspected the remaining plants, of which there were only a few. A few days later the chain pegs were replaced by long metal stakes, needless to say the goats did not escape again.

The Storm

The leaves were falling off the trees in the strong breeze as Master and I walked along the river. They were falling into the water and floating away, it was great fun chasing them. We walked to Cutlers Green and back to Thaxted via the old railway line. It was a lovely sunny day but as the breeze increased the clouds were scudding across the sky. As we got back the sun was setting and, as the light faded, I curled up in my basket and slept.

I awoke later to a howling coming from outside. Lyn came through to the kitchen and opened the back door, and I was hit by a blast of wind. I went out onto the lawn and the noise was incredible - I had never experienced anything like this before. Lyn had followed me out and stood and looked around. I heard the phone ring and soon afterwards Master came rushing out. He was not in uniform but after speaking briefly to Lyn he called me out into the yard. I jumped into the police car and off we went with the roof lights flashing and siren blaring, roaring up the road in the dark. I clung on for dear life as we went around corners, but the 'Police Stop' roller blind fixed to the back shelf stopped me from sliding too far.

After a short distance we arrived at an avenue of trees lining both sides of the road and came to an abrupt halt in front of a huge tree that lay across the road. We got out and the wind hit us both, but it was the noise of the wind hitting the trees with their leaves still on that was really deafening - and quite frightening. Master was shouting on the radio to make himself heard whilst I investigated some interesting scents. A fox had passed through here quite recently, its scent was strong on the road and in the undergrowth nearby. I squeezed under the tree to the other side just as a set of headlights came up towards me. The car slowed down and stopped. Master called me back and I crawled back under the tree. Master spoke to the driver who turned the car around and drove off. This happened several more times with cars arriving from both directions. Suddenly we heard a sound like thunder as another tree came crashing down but this one fell amongst the trees and not across the road.

A few minutes later a truck arrived and drew up behind the police car. Two men got out. They spoke to Master and then went back to the truck and brought back a machine that they started up. It made a tremendous sound, even above the wind, and they started cutting up the tree. Master placed me back in the car and I watched from the front seat as the men and Master slowly cleared the tree away. Within a short while the road was clear and the cut up tree was in the back of the truck. We then left.

Master spoke on the radio - immediately the flashing roof light was back on and we were chasing around the lanes again, I sat firmly on the front seat! We eventually stopped in front of another fallen tree and there were a number of people wandering around. Master got out but I was told to stay in the car. I sat and watched from the front seat. The people who were already there helped Master to lift the tree off the road and soon afterwards we left. Although I had not got out I knew that the wind was still increasing for while Master was out sorting the tree I could feel the car shaking in the wind.

We popped into Saffron Walden Police Station where Master had a cup of tea with his colleagues and one of them gave me a biscuit; I liked him! We were not there for long before Master ran out of the police station with me hot on his heels. We were soon back in the police car speeding off with the roof lights flashing again. I clung on in the front seat as we roared around the lanes for quite a while, this was really exciting. Eventually we came to a stop at a tree which had fallen across the road, but on the other side a car had crashed into the tree and the front of the car was embedded into it. Behind the car was another vehicle with roof lights flashing, and Master told me that this was an 'ambulance'. I was not too certain what an ambulance did, but I was about to find out.

We got out and went around the tree to the crashed car. The driver was still in the car and was being attended to by the man and woman from the ambulance; he was covered in blood. Eventually, with bandages on his head, the driver was helped from the car and placed on a bed on wheels before being lifted into the back of the ambulance. I tried to get into the ambulance to investigate but I could not get up the steps. I sat and watched as the man and woman tended to the driver and spoke to him. The woman then came out and spoke to me and patted my head, I liked her. She got into the front of the ambulance and it then left. I went back to Master who was looking at the smashed car. Soon after the ambulance had gone the two men in the truck that had cut up the other tree earlier arrived and started cutting up this tree. As they did so a further vehicle turned up with a strange contraption on the back. The driver got out and spoke to Master, then hooked up the crashed car to the contraption on the back of his truck and pulled the car out from the tree. A few minutes later the wrecked car was taken way by the truck. The tree was cleared into the back of the other truck and the two men left. We got back into the police car and Master sat there for quite a while writing. I licked his hand and we eventually left.

Master told me that we were 'going home to bed', which I fully understood of course, but our plans were soon dashed when Master got yet another call on the radio. We were off again with the roof lights flashing. We didn't go far before we found a huge tree across a road leading into Thaxted. But this tree had done something different - as it had fallen it had brought down the electricity cables, which were sparking as they hit each other and swayed in the wind above the tree. The flashes were huge and lit up the night sky. Master reversed the car back a short distance and got out. I was told to "stay". He was, however, soon back in the car and talking on the radio as he reversed back a lot further.

Another police car arrived on the other side and we sat there for the rest of the night. Master had to get out occasionally as cars came up behind us. They turned around and went back the way they had come; they were not going to get past this tree in a hurry. I slept on Master's lap which was nice and warm. He would carefully lift me up and place me on the seat if he needed to get out, but I was soon back on his lap when he came back in. As dawn broke another police car pulled up behind us and Master spoke to his colleagues, we then left and returned home. The road home was covered in debris from tree branches to dustbins, roof tiles and all manner of rubbish. Several times Master had to get out and clear the road but eventually we made it home.

As we arrived in the back yard it was quite obvious when I leapt out of the car that my home had not escaped the force of the wind. The side gate had lost all its panels and we stepped straight through the gate frame into the back garden. The wall that had separated our garden from next door had blown over onto our lawns - there were bricks and rubble everywhere - three or four roof tiles also lay smashed on the lawn. Lyn greeted us when we got in and Master had a cup of tea and breakfast with Lyn before going to bed. I slept and dreamt of giant trees and huge sparking cables.

However, our work had not stopped, for mid morning Master and I were back out dealing with all manner of wind damage from fallen trees to collapsed sheds, on the roads all around Thaxted. At one point a caravan had been lifted by the wind over a hedge and had disintegrated on the road. Apart from a quick bite to eat at lunch time at home, we were out all day. Many of the roads were still blocked when we finished but Master had had enough. I slept very well that night and I am sure that Master did as well! The date was the 16th/17th October 1987 and is one which many will remember.

Behind Bars

One morning I took Lyn for a walk along the river. It was a beautiful sunny day with a gentle breeze. There were a lot of water voles to chase, but of course I could not catch them. The remainder of the day was fairly quiet, I sat out on the lawn and played with the flies that were on the grass, they really are very difficult to catch! Master was out. Later in the day I sat on Lyn's lap on the settee but was removed rather abruptly when Master returned. I greeted him as he spoke to Lyn. He disappeared upstairs and came down in his uniform; I got all excited. He sat with Lyn, Phil and Gina at the dining table and ate a meal. The smell from the table was delicious and I lay on Master's feet in case he dropped anything but as usual he didn't, and neither did anyone else.

As darkness fell Master went through to the office and I followed, I wasn't going to let him out of my sight in case we went out in the police car. He sat in there for ages whilst I lay on his feet. Eventually he got up to go and walked to the office door but as he opened it the phone went. I leapt out and ran around to the police car and sat and waited whilst Master answered the phone. He then came rushing out, slammed the office door and ran to the police car. I leapt in and had just got up onto the back shelf when we shot out of the yard with the roof light flashing and the siren wailing. We raced off up the road and through Thaxted.

Soon we came upon an accident involving three cars, all three were badly smashed and one was on fire. The fire brigade had already arrived and were putting the fire out, behind them I could see two ambulances and a lot of people running around. Master had got out and I was told to "stay". I watched from the front seat. More and more vehicles turned up with flashing roof lights. There were a lot of beds on wheels being pushed around. I watched Master and another person climb into one of the cars and help a person out with blood coming from his head. He was put on to one of the beds on wheels and then disappeared into one of the ambulances. I lost sight of Master for a long time, but eventually the vehicles with the flashing roof lights began to disappear and the cars were taken away.

Master eventually came back to the car, spoke for a long time on the radio, and then we left. I wanted to answer the call of nature and I whined at Master. He got the message and stopped in a field gateway and let me out. We then drove to Saffron Walden Police Station where Master had a cup of tea with his colleagues. I went for a wander as usual around the offices. There were some interesting scents around the building but one in particular was worth further investigation as it smelt like food!

I wandered down to the area where the bars were and I managed to squeeze through. As usual one of the doors within was open and it was from this 'cell' that the smell of food was coming, I crept in. There was a man laid out on the bench with a blanket over him, he was snoring loudly. On the floor was a plate of partially eaten pie and chips with peas and a lot of gravy, the meal was still warm. The man had eaten very little of it; he had obviously left it for me! I crept over to the plate and tucked in quietly, keeping one eye on the man. The meal was absolutely delicious and within a very short time I was licking the plate clean of the gravy, I had not spilt a drop. I licked my lips, turned about and waddled out into the corridor. I had eaten so much that my sides were aching, but it was worth it.

I heard the sounds of people moving around upstairs and thought that Master must be on the move. I went up to the bars to squeeze back through, but my very full stomach had swollen up so much so that I could not get back through the bars. I squeezed, pushed, wriggled and tried everything to get through but nothing worked. I was trapped.

I sat and whined to attract Master's attention but he did not appear. I barked loudly several times and eventually I saw Master appear. I wagged my tail in excitement but the tone of Master's voice soon brought me to heel and I sat quietly looking up at him. Another man appeared with a key and the barred gate was opened. I crept out and sat at Master's feet looking up at him, he was not happy, that was obvious by the tone of his voice. We had a very quiet journey home.

The Spikey Creature and the Fleas

One evening I had taken Master for a walk. We had walked down to Dave and Grace's where we had found Dave working in his garden and Grace sitting in a chair by her back door. I was given a biscuit by Grace as Dave and Master talked. It was a lovely evening and on our way back we had a rummage through all the long grass and scrub in the area around the back where Clare Court would eventually be built.

Master had his camera and was photographing some curious insects that he called 'butterflies', while I went off and investigated in the deep grass. Suddenly I came across a curious creature covered in spines.

As I approached, it suddenly curled up into a ball which startled me. I barked and jumped back, its head had disappeared! I was not too sure about this creature and barked at it. Master told me to be quiet but I was too excited. I crept in closer and sniffed at it. I touched it with my nose, which I soon found was a really was a silly thing to do. I yelped in pain and licked my nose, I could taste blood. I was determined to investigate it further and threw caution to the wind. I tried to roll it over to see what was underneath and despite the pain from those needle sharp spines I managed to turn it over but was disappointed to discover that it was the same on the other side. However, I was not going to give up and it was obvious that Master was not going to help me. I placed a paw on it and withdrew it quickly in pain. I sniffed it again and suddenly became aware that I had a 'visitor' under my fur, I began to scratch.

I sat and scratched all over, I appeared to be covered in irritating little visitors. Suddenly the ball began to open which startled me. I watched as a pointed nose and a face appeared from under the spines. My visitors got the better of me and I started scratching again. This startled the little creature who curled up again. I barked again and this time Master came over, and laughed when he saw what I had found. Then he looked at me as I scratched frantically, my visitors were really beginning to irritate me. Master placed my lead on and I was reluctantly led away and taken home, I was rather unceremoniously placed in the kitchen sink and washed from head to foot with a revolting smelling shampoo. I was rinsed off twice and my little visitors were flushed down the sink. As Master washed me I think he could sense that I was not happy. He said to me "That will teach you to play with a hedgehog". But I got my own back for as he was about to lift me out of the sink, I shook myself hard, and the water went all over him!

'Chester'

One morning I awoke and I had a strange feeling. A stirring insidc me was turning my thoughts towards finding a boyfriend. As the days went by, these stirrings got stronger and stronger. Behind our house there was some building work being carried out, and one of the workmen had a very handsome Staffordshire Bull Terrier. He was dark brown and very stocky. His name was 'Chester' and he was gorgeous! He would walk his Master past our back gate and I would watch him through a small hole in the wooden fence. He would sniff the air and look in my direction, and I would get really excited.

One morning after breakfast I was out on the back lawn when I heard a loud sniffing from the gate. I rushed over and could just see Chester's nose under the narrow gap at the bottom of the gate, our noses met. Chester was whimpering softly and with his broad, powerful jaws he started chewing at the bottom of the gate. The wood was pretty rotten and within a short space of time there was a loud sound of splintering wood as the hole grew bigger and bigger. His head appeared through the hole and we greeted each other. Soon he was through the gate and we ran around the garden in our excitement. He really was a handsome dog - broad and solid. His front legs were slightly bowed as we stood and looked at each other, and then suddenly we burst into a run, him chasing me before the roles were reversed, this was great fun. He wanted me and I wanted him.

Our fun was short lived when the kitchen door burst open and Master came rushing out, shouting at us. I was picked up and carried indoors with Chester jumping up at me. I was placed rather unceremoniously into my basket and the kitchen door was slammed shut. Master's body language led me to believe that he was not at all happy. I heard Master shouting outside in the garden as Lyn watched on from the kitchen window.

Later the same day, I was taken to the vet where I was given a very painful injection, which only confirmed my belief that vets really are nasty people. It was dark when we got home. Chester's scent was still on the lawn but the hole in the gate had been blocked up. I never saw Chester again.

The Canal

One day, after a very early morning walk, we all got into the car and we were off somewhere. I sat across Phil and Gina's laps for a while but eventually ended up in my usual place, up on the back shelf, where I went into a deep sleep.

When I awoke we were parked in a car park next to a small road bridge which went over a long stretch of water. There were some interesting scents in the car park, including a partly eaten sandwich that went down a treat!

We walked off along a path that ran close to and parallel to the water that glistened and sparkled in the bright sunlight, the strong breeze whipping up the waves. The sunlight flickered and danced on the surface. We passed under the road-bridge and approached a second bridge that towered above us. Against the opposite bank as we approached the bridge there were some curious boats moored up. They were very long.

As we began to pass under this huge bridge there was a sudden, loud, frightening, thunderous sound coming from the roof. It startled and terrified me. I ran off flat out, clearing the bridge as the sound faded away. Lyn spoke to me laughing as she explained to me that it was a 'train' going over. Whatever it was I didn't like it!

We walked away from this bridge, passing another curious bridge that also spanned the river. We all walked onto it and stood and looked at the water that Master explained to me was a 'canal'. He also explained that the bridge we were standing on was called a 'swing bridge' to get sheep and cattle from one side of the canal to the other.

He then went to the other side and started pushing it. The bridge moved with us on it, a strange feeling that I didn't like. Eventually we ended up on one side of the water, on the opposite side to the path we had been walking along. Phil and Gina were laughing and running up and down the bridge. Master then swung the bridge back across the water and I ran back onto the path.

We walked on along the path and came to a cottage next to the path, behind a high hedge. Master and Lyn stopped and looked over the hedge. Master had his camera and I ran on ahead with Phil and Gina. We stopped at two sets of strange gates that spanned the canal, with a long gap between each pair of gates. This gap was a deep chasm. Master and Lyn caught up with us just as one of the curious long boats approached the gates from the lower end. Master explained to me and the kids that this was a 'lock'.

There was a woman at one end of the boat and a man approaching us along the path. The boat slowly entered the deep lock as the man reached us. I stood and watched, fascinated by what was going on. I had also spotted a dog like me asleep on the flat roof of the boat.

Once in the lock the man closed the gate on our side and then walked to the closed gates at the other end, walked across them and back up towards us to close the other gate. He then walked to the other end again and started winding something with a curious contraption. This in turn created a thunderous sound from within the lock which frightened me. The man then walked back across the gates to our side and started winding again, This increased the thunderous roar from within the lock and looking down I could see where the sound was coming from as water was cascading into the lock. After a short time I could see that the boat in the lock was slowly rising towards us. The dog on the roof had awoken and was sitting up looking at me, he was a handsome individual!

The lock was soon full of water and the boat was on a level with us. The woman spoke to us as the man opened the gate on the opposite bank. Master opened the gate on our side and the man jumped aboard the boat as it chugged out of the lock towards the swing bridge. I barked a greeting at the dog and he barked back at me. The woman and man waved as the boat moved off along the canal.

There was a bench nearby and everyone sat down and started to eat some food. I sat at their feet hoping to get a morsel but I didn't so I went off and investigated some interesting scents in the long grass behind the bench - I did get a bowl of water though!

After a long rest there we began to walk further along the canal, eventually reaching another road-bridge with boats moored up either side. There was a pub next to the bridge with a number of people sitting outside at tables. I was placed on my lead and we sat outside next to the water. Master disappeared inside only to return with a tray with glasses on and some packets. I recognised these as containing delicious treats, and if I was lucky I might get some - I did!

We stayed there quite a while before moving off back along the path to the lock and the cottage beyond where Master stopped for a while. Lyn and the others walked on. I stayed with Master. He told me that this cottage and farm were owned by his 'grandfather' and it was here that he 'grew up' and he regarded it as 'home'. Although I did not understand a word of it I did get the impression that this was a very special place to him.

We passed very quickly under the huge bridge but it remained quiet. Back at the car we were soon on the road again and I was sound asleep. It was dark when I woke in the back yard of the police house.

Snowed In

It was the time of the year when the tree comes into the house and funny lights are put on it, I believe it is called 'Christmas'. Lots of people came and went and everyone had a good time. I was given a new squeeze ball that gave out a shrill whistle every time I bit it. The challenge for me was to get the whistle out of the ball and of course it did not take me long. John, Kath, Marc and Faith stayed for a few days and John and Master took me for long walks which I thoroughly enjoyed.

Soon after they left we were off in the car early one morning and it soon became apparent to me that this was going to be a long journey. Phil and Gina were in the back with one of Phil's mates, David Wiffen. They were all asleep in the back and I slept up on the back shelf. Eventually some familiar scents entered the car which woke me up, there were regular scents from around the cottage, but the dominant scent was that of the sea. I got excited and jumped down onto David's lap.

We stopped outside the front door of the cottage and we all piled out of the car. The weather was very dull and there was a bitterly cold wind blowing. Master unloaded the car with Dave and Phil's help. Lyn lit the fire and we were soon all sitting around the flames which warmed up the room. My favourite place was laying out right in front of the fire, boy did it get hot there, and within a short while I had to move away to cool off only to return and 'cook' soon after.

Much later we all went down to the pub in the village for a meal. The wind had got up outside and there were one or two snowflakes in the wind. There was a roaring fire in the pub and our table was right near it. I sat under the table ready to snaffle up any bits that dropped onto the floor but there were none for me that day. After the warmth of the pub the wind outside hit me with a blast. I winced and screwed up my eyes. The snow was falling heavily and horizontally in the gale force wind. It seemed like a long walk back to the cottage, but it was lovely to scamper into the nice warm room. I was soon ensconced back in front of the fire, my wet coat steaming in heat. My basket was in the kitchen and at bed time the boys slept downstairs once their bed had been blown up, Gina was in her own room.

The following morning there was an air of excitement in the cottage but I was not certain why. After breakfast Master stoked the fire up. Everyone put their coats, boots and hats on, and the front door opened. Everybody laughed for there was a wall of snow piled up against the door. The snow had blown into the porch on the wind and had drifted against the door. The drift had been half way up the door, and some had fallen into the cottage when the door opened. Lyn and Master cleared the snow out of the cottage while Phil, David and Gina walked through the wall of snow out onto what had been the road beyond, but was now just a white expanse. I followed them - this was great fun. They started throwing balls of snow at each other and at me, and I caught one or two. The snow was deeper than I was and it was hard work running through the snow with my short legs.

Gina fell over in the snow and was laughing when I reached her and licked her but she was soon back on her feet, throwing snow at the lads. With a shovel, Master cleared a path through the snow from the door to the road.

Later I took everyone for a walk. Very little traffic used this road on a normal day and now there were none - we were effectively cut off. We walked up to the church. The lads were throwing balls of snow at Master and Lyn who were of course retaliating. As we walked down the track to the church, David and Phil started jumping into the deep snow drifts in what had been ditches.

I jumped in on top of them – boy, this was exciting. Once or twice we completely disappeared under the snow that collapsed in over us. When we had started the walk the snow had stopped though it was still very dull. By the time we eventually reached the church, the snow was falling again and the settled snow was blowing off the fields in our path. As I was so low it was stinging my face. We walked on past the church and along the track towards a bridge over the railway line, which ran from Walsingham to Wells-Next-The-Sea. There were no hedges on either side of the track, just vast open fields. With the snow falling and blowing off the fields it was much deeper and very difficult for me. Thankfully Master and Lyn decided to turn around before we reached the bridge and we walked back to the cottage.

By the time we got back the snow was falling heavily and it was nice to be back in the warm cottage. I was soon back in my favourite spot in front of the fire. Gina was standing next to me shaking her gloves over the fire, when they suddenly slipped out of her hands and into the roaring flames. By the time anybody could do anything they were well alight. Gina was very upset.

Much later in the day I joined Phil, Gina and David in the back garden which was a raised garden and was deep in snow. They built a man out of the snow by rolling up huge balls of snow, with my help of course! His eyes and mouth were pieces of clinker from previous fires and his nose was a carrot, what a waste of a lovely carrot! I went into a deep sleep in front of the fire, but not too close. Later we went to bed, the boys sleeping on the floor again. It was nice and warm in there and as the kitchen door had been left open I crept in and snuggled up to Phil on his duvet in front of the fire, this was sheer luxury.

The following morning after breakfast, I took everyone for a walk. There was another huge snow drift in the porch of the front door which the lads crashed through, followed of course by me. It had stopped snowing but there was a gale force wind blowing and the snow was blowing horizontally. It was very cold, so cold in fact that it stung my eyes. We walked down into the village and past the school playground where our car was parked. It was completely buried in snow, just a huge lump in the middle of the white desert that was a playground. The boys used it for target practice, dislodging some of the snow on the side of it. I was now well out of my depth in the snow and it was quite hard work moving through it but good fun. There was an eerie silence - no traffic and no-one out and about - Wighton is a very small village. We eventually climbed the long hill back up to the cottage where the fire was very welcoming. Later I examined the 'snowman' in the back garden, he was partially buried in fresh snow but his face was still clearly recognisable. I tried to get the carrot by jumping up, but without success!

Later in the day I went back out with the boys, it was still very overcast and it was getting dark. The wind continued to blow and it had become very cold, I screwed my eyes up. We had some fun in the lane leading to the church. On one occasion I disappeared in a snow drift that had formed by the snow blowing off the fields. The boys jumped in either side of me and Phil reached in the drift and pulled me out by the scruff of my neck, of course I would have crawled out eventually, wouldn't I?

The strange silence continued, the only sound was the boys laughing. We eventually returned in the pitch dark to the cottage and I curled up in front of the fire.

The next few days were much the same; more snow fell and we remained cut off.

We all helped the tiny village shop next door deliver some tins of food to a few of the cottages in the village. This was great fun for me, as it gave me a chance to investigate the front gardens of many of the cottages, but of course there was not a lot to scent out because of the deep snow. Master, Lyn and the others either ate in the cottage in the evening or we trudged down to the pub - I believe Master called it 'The Sandpiper' - where they all ate. I sat in front of the huge fire which was much bigger than the one in the cottage. The odd chip or scrap of food would come my way, courtesy of the boys or Gina!

One morning, after breakfast I took everyone for a walk and we had just reached the road when I heard a loud machine moving towards the village from the direction of Wells. This was the first vehicle I had heard for some time. Eventually the noise got louder and louder, and suddenly it burst through the deep snow that was as high as Master, in front of us. The front of the machine, which Master called a 'snow plough', was covered in bright lights which glared in the dull light.

It also had a number of roof lights that were flashing brightly. The monster of a machine had a chute high to one side and snow was shooting out of it onto the fields. It passed us and then turned down into the village and past the cottage.

The channel that it left behind was as wide as one car, but there was still a lot of snow on the road. Master stood in the channel and the top of the wall of snow was up to his head. It towered over me. Eventually the machine came back up the road in front of the cottage and then turned off towards Walsingham with the chute spreading the snow into the fields, and leaving a narrow channel with high snow walls either side. As the machine slowly disappeared around a bend, the snow began falling again as the daylight faded. We returned to the cottage via the track made by the machine. It was very slippery, and the lads had great fun sliding down the hill but my claws stopped me from sliding.

That night we walked/slipped down to the pub. Master slipped over twice and by the tone of his voice he was not very happy. Getting back up the hill after the meal was interesting; of course I had no trouble with my claws. The humans all linked arms and helped each other up, laughing and giggling. The thin layer of snow that had fallen after the snow plough had gone through made the track very difficult to walk on. I slept very well that night with Phil and David in front of the fire.

The following morning everyone was up early and there was an air of excitement in the air. Master had not stoked the fire up as he normally did but had spent some time clearing the fireplace out. Cases were brought down from upstairs and left by the front door. Eventually Master went outside and I followed him.

It was bright sunlight outside, which dazzled me as it glared off of the snow. We walked down to the playground where the car was and he spent more time clearing all the snow off the car. He threw a ball of snow at me which I tried to catch but it merely exploded in my mouth. Eventually we got into the car and it started. We slowly drove out of the playground and up to the front door of the cottage. I remained up on the back shelf when Master got out; I was not going to be left behind! The boot of the car was loaded and eventually everyone got in and we were off.

We drove out of the road outside the cottage and into the road where the really deep snow was. We drove along the channel made by the snow plough and all I could see was a wall of snow on either side of the car. We were travelling very slowly. Once or twice we met cars coming towards us which meant that we had to reverse back to a spot where the snow plough had cleared a slightly wider channel where cars could pass. I went to sleep up on the shelf and woke quite a while later and looked out of the window. There was no snow at all, not a hint of it and this remained the same all the way back to Thaxted; it was nice to be home.

David's parents called around to collect him and I slept well that night dreaming of giant snow drifts!

Bismark

Once a year there was a lot of activity at the police house, which culminated in the Thaxted Fayre weekend. During the weeks leading up to the fayre there was a lot of comings and goings and meetings. I got to know most of the people there.

Eventually the weekend arrived. I took Master and Gina for a walk down to Dave and Grace's and Master left me there whilst he took Gina to school. I was spoilt as usual with two biscuits. Master collected me and we walked off in a different direction to usual. We walked through two small housing estates and ended up in the recreation ground where there was a lot of activity. Master let me off the lead and I went off to investigate, but Master soon called me back as there were lorries everywhere. Huge canvas 'buildings' were going up - Master called them 'marquees'. Master spoke to several people there and I then took him home. He was in and out of the house with Lyn for the rest of the day while I stayed in my basket. That evening a number of police officers arrived in the office and after I had greeted them I was turned out into the hallway - I was not happy. Lyn was popping in and out of the office with trays of teas and coffees so I retired to my bed. Even from my bed I could hear the sound of loud music coming from the recreation ground and a lot of voices out on the road. Eventually I heard voices in the office and Master and Lyn came through into the house leaving the office door open. I scurried through and greeted everyone. They made a big fuss of me, I liked them! More trays of teas and coffees went through and they all sat talking whilst I sat on Master's lap. Later everybody left and the office lights were turned out. I went to bed, it had been a busy day.

The following morning Lyn and Master were up early, and after breakfast I took Master for a walk up to the recreation ground. There were two huge marquees and loads of small ones. There were interesting scents everywhere, especially food on the grass. There were bits of burgers and sausages all over the place. Although Master tried to stop me eating them by keeping me on my lead, they were too good to miss!

We were walking along the side of one of the big marquees when I suddenly became aware of a dog on the other side of the canvas inside the marquee. I became very curious and started sniffing the bottom of the canvas where the wall of the marquee met the ground. We sniffed each other and I formed the opinion that this dog was bigger than me and worthy of further investigation - this was a strange dog on my territory. However Master had other ideas and I was pulled away, my day would come. We left the recreation ground and I led Master through the field opposite which was down to stubble and stung my tummy. There were a number of cars parked there and we passed them before eventually arriving at the river where I had a swim. I was still dripping when we got home and Lyn dried me off with a towel, I enjoyed that.

There was a lot of coming and going in the house and office throughout the day and I couldn't sleep. As dusk fell, the office filled with people and Lyn was busy with teas and coffees again. The music had started up at the recreation ground and there were crowds of people walking on the road past the office towards the music. I tried to sleep but the noise kept me awake. It continued for quite some time, spoiling my beauty sleep. Eventually it stopped and some time later I heard the office door open and voices. I scuttled through to see who had come in; it was Master, Lyn and a few policemen. Lyn came through and spoke briefly to the policemen, who then left. Master came through and said good night to me, and then he and Lyn went to bed.

The following morning everybody was up early. I took Lyn and Master up to the recreation ground and as yesterday there was a lot of food lying around. At the marquee I sensed the dog at the canvas again but this time I was determined to discover who this intruder on my 'patch' was and send him packing if necessary. I sniffed the canvas and I could hear the other dog sniffing on the other side. This got my hackles up and I barked loudly. At this point both Lyn and Master called me back but I ignored them, I was determined to see this intruder off once and for all. I barked aggressively at the canvas and the dog inside barked back, his voice deep and menacing. Near to me was a strip down the side of the marquee running from top to bottom. This strip was laced up. I sniffed at the strip - I knew the other dog was on the other side. I barked aggressively again and pulled hard at the laces. At this point I could hear Master approaching and by the tone of his voice he was not happy.

I barked again and suddenly there was a bark from within, that sounded like thunder, the ground shook below my paws. This was followed immediately by a huge crash against the side of the marquee at the point where the laces were. I say were because they flew open from top to bottom and there, standing in the gap, was a huge monster of a dog. He was the biggest dog I have ever seen - my entire body would have fitted in his mouth! He towered over me and gave out a thunderous bark but I was gone. I shot between Lyn and Master and ran like the wind across the recreation ground. It was the fastest I had ever run and I was certain that those huge jaws were going to close over my body at any minute. I could hear Master and Lyn calling but if I stopped I would certainly be eaten. I dared not look behind as this would have certainly sealed my fate. I ran and ran until I reached the hedge on the other side where, still running, I sneaked a look behind me expecting the monster to be about to devour me, but he was nowhere to be seen.

I stopped, panting heavily and looked across the recreation ground to the marquee where I could see the monster still sitting in the doorway of the marquee that he had opened. He had not shifted from the spot where I first saw him! I stood there for quite a while until Master walked over to where I was standing and called me a silly girl then placed me on my lead. We walked back across the recreation ground giving the marquee a wide berth. My eyes were on the monster the entire time. 'Bismarck' the Rottweiller was a guard dog who had been employed with his Master to guard the contents of this marquee, which housed amongst other things the bar!

The Rat

Master and I were out one evening for a walk. We had walked down to Dave and Grace's where Dave was working in his garden as usual. While Master and Dave talked I crept off down the path to the back door which was open and inside I found Grace sitting in her armchair. I greeted her by wagging my tail and licking her, I was hoping for a biscuit. She got up and walked out to the kitchen while I followed close on her heels. She picked up a tin which I knew from previous visits had treats in. She made me say please as usual - this consisted of a little yelp – and I was rewarded with a biscuit which was delicious. She gave me a second, I was being spoilt, and then I followed her down the garden to join the others.

We eventually left and walked to the church and to the windmill beyond. It was a lovely evening with the sun setting on the horizon at Cutlers Green. We walked down to the river and along the path in the general direction of home. There was a strong scent of rats coming from the stubble on the side of the path and from the river bank. Master was in no hurry and was walking quite slowly. He had his camera around his neck and kept stopping to take photographs, whatever they are.

Suddenly a huge rat ran out of the stubble across the path in front of me. I darted forward and grabbed the rat just behind the neck. A quick bite and a flick of my head and its lifeless body landed at Master's feet. He reached down to pick it up but I beat him to it. I grabbed it and ran off along the path with my 'prize' in my jaws; its head hung out of one side of my mouth and its body and tail out of the other. Master called me back and tried to get my prize from me but I was having none of that. He called me again with a very stern voice but I ignored him. I kept a good distance ahead of him and could hear him muttering something. By the tone it was obviously aimed at me although I pretended not to hear him.

Eventually we arrived home and I still had my prize. Lyn was in the kitchen when I went in but she took one look at me and the rat and ran out slamming the inner kitchen door as she did so I got into my basket and sat there with the rat in my jaws. What was I going to do with it now? Master went to a cupboard and I heard the familiar sound of the dog biscuit bag. I put the rat down, jumped out of the basket and sat at Master's feet looking up at him. Master threw the biscuit across the kitchen floor, I chased after it and ate it in one go. Master said I "didn't deserve it" what ever that meant. A second biscuit was thrown down and when I took it back to my basket the rat had gone. Master had won. I was to kill many more rats during my life but Lyn never liked them!

A New Addition to the Family

One morning there was an air of excitement in the house. Everyone was busy doing this and that, Phil and Gina were busy upstairs and by the crashing and banging going on it sounded like furniture was being moved. After breakfast I took Master for a very quick walk down to the river. When we got back there was a strange car in the back yard and there was a strong scent of Marc. I rushed indoors and there he was sitting on the settee. I took a flying jump and landed on his lap, immediately licking his face. He made a big fuss of me which I loved of course. Everyone laughed as I snuggled in by the side of him, Master looked at me but didn't say anything.

Marc had been visiting us over the past few weeks on a fairly regular basis, and here he was again. Everyone sat around talking for a while before Master got up and helped Marc unload his car. Cases and boxes galore were taken upstairs and I sneaked up to see what was going on. All the stuff was going into Phil's room and a second bed by the window had been made up. Marc was busy unloading the boxes and cases and putting stuff into drawers and cupboards. I didn't really understand what was going on and looked a bit puzzled when Master spoke to me and said Marc was 'moving in'. As usual I hadn't got a clue what he meant!

The following morning Marc joined us for breakfast and I sat on his feet. Afterwards I watched him through a crack in the fence as he got into his car and drove off. The day passed quietly with Master and Lyn sitting in the sun in the garden. Much later Marc returned and I greeted him. I sat on his feet under the table during the evening meal and this became the regular routine. After the meal Phil and Marc would take me for a walk, usually along the river. We were often joined by some of their mates, Paul, David, Gerry and Andy, collectively known as 'The Lads'. They would walk along talking and make a fuss of me, which I liked of course.

One morning after breakfast there was a knock at the door and I barked a warning as I ran towards it. Phil opened the door and there were all of the lads ready to make a fuss of me as they came in. They sat around talking in the sitting room then Master said something to them and I recognised two words 'Cassie' and 'Walkies'. I had got so used to the second word that Master started to disguise it by saying "Whisky, Alpha, Lima, Kilo, India, Echo, Sierra". He thought that I did not know what that meant, but I did of course! The lads got up and walked towards the back door. Phil put my lead on and we were off. I was really excited - it was always good fun when the lads were together.

They were all talking as we walked across the field to the river. As soon as we were away from the road Phil took my lead off. We crossed the river and walked along the path. The lads started throwing long strands of grass with soil on the bottom at each other and trying to catch them. If they didn't catch it, I would run in and grab it and run off. They would then chase me but of course I outran them every time, it was good fun. The lads were full of it: bombing each other with the grass, and chasing me or I would chase them. On one occasion Phil fell over and I leapt on top of him and licked his face, he was laughing so much that he couldn't get up.

We walked quite a way along the river to a point where there was a bend with a large bush that overhung the path. I immediately saw a curious creature standing on the path. It saw me and ran off and I gave chase, barking excitedly. The lads were calling me but I ignored them, this was much more fun. At a narrow point in the river the creature ran down the bank and jumped across the water before running up the other bank and disappearing in the undergrowth. I followed but missed the other bank and crashed into the water. I swam to the bank and continued chasing the creature which had disappeared. I ran through some deep vegetation which stung my paws. There was no sign of the animal, and no scent but I continued pushing through the undergrowth. I could hear Marc and Phil calling my name but I ignored them and kept going. Suddenly I came to a small clearing and there straight ahead the animal was standing, facing me. I barked at it, which I immediately discovered was the wrong thing to do. It lowered its head and as I continued barking at this strange animal, it suddenly charged towards me with its head down in a very threatening way. It startled me and I ran off back through the stinging undergrowth. I eventually reached the river and with a giant leap from the top of the bank I flew through the air and crashed down into the water. I quickly swam across the water and ran up the other side straight into Phil's arms. I looked back for the first time since the animal charged at me and expected to see it running at us but there was nothing there. My feet were stinging and I licked them, which seemed to make them worse.

As we walked off Phil told me that it was a Muntjack Deer, all I knew was that I did not like it. We walked all the way up to the old station, where everyone sat down. I jumped on to Phil's lap and licked his face, he fell back laughing. Marc and the others all laughed and I leapt all over them licking their faces, everybody was hysterical.

Eventually I had to sit down to get my breath back. We walked down a track back to the river and passed the building with funny arm that Master once told me was a windmill and the high spire of the church beyond. I went for a swim on the way home to cool off.

These walks with the lads became a fairly regular feature in my life, and I always got excited when they turned up. Marc and Phil would also take me on their own after supper. Master once told me that they walked me to 'get out of the washing up', whatever it meant, it was good news for me!

Police Dogs!

One evening Master was in the office writing at his desk and I was asleep on his feet. It was quite late and Lyn and Gina had gone to bed. Marc and Phil were in the sitting room watching TV, as usual. The phone rang and Master spoke into it. He immediately got up, grabbed his coat and ran out of the office door with me following. It was cold, windy and heavy rain was falling. We jumped into the police car and I climbed up on to the back shelf, which was just as well as the roof lights went on and we shot out of the drive. We were travelling really fast so I sat tight on the shelf – it was the safest place to be when Master was driving at speed. We went through Saffron Walden, and on and on until eventually we came to an abrupt halt outside a church. There were a number of other police cars there and policemen gathered around a smashed up car the front of which was embedded in the front of one of the police cars, oops! The policemen were wearing uniforms that were slightly different to Master's and I later learnt that they were Cambridgeshire officers. Master got out and I followed.

Master spoke to the officers who were all looking at the damage to the police car. Suddenly, through their legs I spotted two enormous German Shepherd dogs, fortunately they were on leads. They brought their handlers over to where Master and I were standing and one of the handlers said to Master, "We knew that Essex Police were making cut-backs, but that is ridiculous", he was pointing at me. They all laughed. The two tracker dogs then went off with their handlers through the churchyard and disappeared into the dark.

A few minutes later the two dogs with their handlers returned with a very dirty, scruffy, wet man walking between them. He looked miserable as he was placed rather unceremoniously into the back of a police car and driven away. We stayed with the others for a while but eventually a huge lorry arrived and the smashed up cars were loaded on to it. We then got back into our car and left. Master explained to me on the way home that the car had been stolen in Cambridge and had been involved in a serious road accident before being chased out of the city into Essex and eventually to the church where the car then rammed the police car in an attempt to get away. The tracker dogs had found the man hiding in the graveyard behind the church. He was in a lot of trouble. Of course I fully understood all this? All I knew was it was great fun.

The Downs

After a very early walk one morning, Master and I were in the car and off on our travels. I sat on the front seat but soon got tired and went to sleep. I woke with an urge to go to the toilet and whined at Master. He pulled over, stopped the car and put my lead on. Once I had finished we were back on the road again and I was soon asleep.

I awoke to the familiar scents of sheep and rabbit drifting into the car. We were in a car park at the base of a hill. Master told me that this was 'Chanctonbury'. I was out of the car like a shot and running up a hedge-lined track. It was a beautiful sunny day and there was a strong breeze. Master grabbed his camera and shut the car door. When he called me back I reluctantly returned and we walked off together.

After a short distance the hedge stopped and we walked across open grass towards a clump of trees in the distance that Master told me was 'Chanctonbury Ring'. I ran on ahead and the air was full of interesting scents. I was really excited and ran back to Master jumping up at him. He patted me on the head and we walked on side by side. As we drew closer to the trees the view opened up all around us and I sat up to get a better view.

When we reached the trees Master sat down on the grass and I sat on his lap. We sat and looked at the countryside that stretched away in front of us and I turned around and licked Master's face. He grabbed me and suspended me in the air as he lay down laughing. I just hung there looking down at him. He placed me down on to the grass and I immediately jumped up onto his chest and licked his face, his beard made me sneeze. He laughed as he tried to brush me away but I was determined to keep licking him, he tasted nice. He suddenly sat up and I tumbled down off him.

He jumped to his feet and chased after me - I ran flat out in a big circle around him - he was going to have to be quick to catch me. I was distracted by a big black bird that landed on the grass near me. I chased after it but it was in the air and away by the time I got near it. When I turned around Master had walked off so I ran after him and hit him in the back of the legs hard, he ignored me.

We walked around to the other side of the ring of trees where we saw a man and a boy with a curious and frightening object flying high in the sky above them. I barked loudly and ran back to Master, keeping close to his legs. I barked again and again to get the thing to go away, but it just hung there. Master told me that it was alright and that it was 'only a kite'. Whatever it was I did not like it and I was glad when we moved away from it, after Master had spoken to the people briefly. I ran on ahead to get away from the strange 'creature'.

I was investigating an interesting rabbit scent when I suddenly became aware that Master was creeping up behind me I went to move but he grabbed me in his huge hands and swung me high into the air above him. He held me there and I looked down on his smiling face. He lowered me down and gave me a big hug. I licked his hand as he lowered me down on to the short grass. As we walked away from the trees we had a game of chase. I led him a merry run but he didn't catch me and by the time we got back to the car we were both panting heavily. I was given a bowl of water, boy I was thirsty.

We left the car park and went down into the town that Master called Worthing where we met up with two women that I had met before. Two big cases were placed in the boot of the car and the women got in. We had a long drive home to Thaxted and I went into a deep sleep on the back shelf. It was dark when I got out in the back yard and after greeting Lyn and the kids, I curled up in my box and slept, dreaming of the downs and monsters in the sky!

Snow and 'The Lads'

It was just after the time when a tree comes into the house and there is lots of activity going on, I believe it is called 'Christmas'. It was very cold outside and there was ice on the river. One morning Master was in bed having worked all night. Lyn and I had taken Gina to school, via Dave and Grace's of course, Phil was out and Marc had left for work, early as usual. I decided to take Lyn for a walk along the river.

There was a bitterly cold wind blowing and the sky was overcast. We reached the river which had completely frozen over. It felt quite strange as I ran nervously across the ice from one side to the other. It was slippery underfoot and I had to use my claws to get a grip, even so once or twice I went down on my face. The ground was also frozen hard. As we walked it began to snow, initially just light flakes carried virtually horizontally in the wind but by the time we got home it was very heavy and the ground was turning white. It was nice and warm indoors out of the wind.

Later I went out onto the lawn where the snow was already up to my tummy and still falling heavily. Master had gone out on foot and returned with a huge vehicle that filled the back yard, or so it seemed. Master told me that it was a Land Rover and that he had borrowed it to deal with the snow. Although I did not know what this meant, over the next few days I soon found out. By early evening Master and I were out in the Land Rover pulling stranded cars up the hill near our house. The snow was really deep and continued to fall. We would drive down to the bottom of the long hill, hitch up the next car in the traffic jam at the bottom with a rope and pull them to the top where the rope was untied. I had a good view of what was going on from the windows in the back of the Land Rover and the long seats that ran under the window.

One of the cars we pulled up was Marc's, and we towed him from the top of the hill the short distance home. We parked his car up and he rushed indoors only to reappear shortly afterwards with Phil. They jumped into the back of the Land Rover with me and we returned to pulling cars up the hill, it was really quite exciting. We had been joined by other Land Rovers and we quickly cleared the jam. No more cars came through as the road was now blocked. We went for a drive around the roads of Thaxted and found they were all blocked. There were several cars in ditches and the boys got out each time to check that there was no one in them.

At one car we met a lady who appeared to be very upset and Master got out. Her car was completely submerged in the deep snow in a ditch. Master, along with Phil and Marc, set to work trying to clear the snow around the door with the shovel that we had on board. Marc let me out but the snow was really deep and I had a job moving through it. Phil was holding a torch while Master and Marc cleared the snow and managed to open the door. Master climbed into the car that was lying partially on its side in the snow. He disappeared into the car and re-emerged shortly after with a tiny dog that looked petrified - it was a Chihuahua. Master handed it to the woman, whose relief was quite evident. The lady with her dog climbed into the front passenger seat and Marc, Phil and I got in the back (Phil lifted me in as there was no way that I could jump in that high!) We took the lady home as she lived in a nearby village.

On the way back we came across another car in a ditch just as the snow started to fall heavily again. This time an elderly gentleman was standing nearby. Master got out and helped the man into the Land Rover; he was shivering badly and appeared to be quite distressed. We took him back to the police house where the lads helped him into the lounge. Lyn gave him a cup of tea and wrapped a big blanket around him. We then took him home to Saffron Walden. The road was really interesting as there were cars abandoned everywhere and driving around them was quite a challenge. I now knew why Master had commandeered the Land Rover! We delivered the man to his house and a lady was waiting at the door as Marc and Phil helped him down the path.

We drove back the way we came, stopping and checking each abandoned vehicle to make sure that there was no one inside - this was Marc and Phil's job - I watched out of the side windows. We eventually reached home and as we went into the house the snow and wind was increasing. Needless to say I dreamt of giant snow drifts!

The following morning the snow was so deep that the steps out of the kitchen door had disappeared and I stepped out straight onto the snow. I had great fun moving around on the snow that glistened and dazzled in the bright sunlight. After breakfast we were all out in the back garden and it soon became apparent why. The kids were building what I now know as was 'snowman'. It was huge and had big eyes and a carrot for a nose. What a waste - I love carrots.

After that Phil and Marc piled into the back of the Land Rover with me and we were joined by Gerry and Andy - nobody was going to work or school that day. I sat on Marc's lap in the front with Master. Nothing was moving on the roads, which was hardly surprising in view of the depth of the snow. There were a lot of people walking around and Master tried to explain to me that Thaxted was 'cut off', whatever that meant.

We went out to some of the villages around Thaxted and the lads jumped out a number of times to help people clearing the snow from their paths. Master also called in on a number of elderly people checking that they were okay. We were out for most of the day but as darkness fell we returned home. After their meal Phil and Marc went out and took me with them.

We walked down to an area known as Piggotts Hill which is a fairly steep hill that runs down to the river. Normally covered in grass it was now a white desert in the moonlight. There were a lot of people there sliding down the hill on all manner of contraptions that I later learnt were 'sledges'. Phil and Marc joined up with some friends and were sliding down the hill on a huge sledge whilst I gave chase - this was good fun. At the bottom they would stop and drag the sledge back up the hill again. Six or seven of them would then jump on and tear down the hill at full speed with me chasing them. On one occasion Marc picked me up and I sat on the sledge with the others. Down we went, Marc holding me firmly. I was so excited I barked out loud. At the bottom we disappeared in a cloud of snow that was kicked up by the front of the sledge.

On the next downhill run Phil held me as we sat on the front of the sledge with all the others behind us. Down we hurtled, the cold wind in our faces. The breeze was so strong that my ears stood up! At the bottom we were at full speed when the sledge suddenly veered sharply and we overturned in the deep snow. Phil and I were catapulted into the air, coming down into a blanket of snow. When I shook myself there were bodies everywhere all laughing out loud, this was excellent fun. After that the lads started to deliberately crash the sledge in the deep snow. Much later we returned home - I for one was tired with all the excitement, the running around and moving through the deep snow with my short legs - I slept well that night.

The following morning it was snowing heavily again. Master was in uniform at breakfast which only meant one thing - we were going out again. After breakfast Master, Phil and Marc got into the Land Rover and I was lifted into the back. There was still no traffic on the roads and we visited a couple of remote houses, but with the snow falling heavily again we returned home.

Later the same day as the light began to fade we all went back down to Piggotts Hill where there were a lot of people sledging. Lyn and Gina joined us with some friends and were sledging down on a small plastic sledges. I stayed with the lads who were on the big one and we had a great time. Master rode down on it as well and he held onto me, as we had several descents. On one occasion we turned over at the bottom and bodies flew in all directions. I landed on top of Master who had partially disappeared in the deep snow, everyone was laughing hysterically.

In addition to the sledging the lads were having a snowball fight and I was having great fun trying to catch them. On one occasion Marc threw one at Master which caught him on the ear. Master was not happy, but he got his own back. Master pushed Marc over into a big snowdrift and threw Phil in after him. I joined in and disappeared in the snow, only to be hauled out by Master's huge hand. Then Phil and Marc and some others ganged up against Master and threw him into a deep snowdrift. He rose out of it looking like the snowman in the garden. His beard had gone white and he was laughing.

We eventually returned home and it felt strange walking down the centre of what had been the road but there was no danger of traffic. Later the same evening, as a result of a phone call, we were back out again. Phil, Marc and I were in the back of the Land Rover. We ploughed through the snow to a cottage on the outskirts of Thaxted and Master disappeared inside. The cottage was in darkness but shortly after Master went in the lights came on. The front door opened and I saw Master talking to a little old lady. He eventually came back to the Land Rover and we left. Master explained to the lads that the old lady had lost all power in her cottage but he was able to rectify the problem. On the way back we met Gerry and Andy and they jumped in the back with us. We drove out into the white countryside and Master stopped the Land Rover by the side of what seemed to be a slight dip in a field. The lads leapt out and to my amazement promptly disappeared. It turned out that the dip was in fact a deep ditch which was full of snow. The lads spent quite a while leaping into the drift so I joined in, this was great fun. I spent more time under the snow than on top of it but the lads kept pulling me out. Snowballs were raining in from all directions. Master joined in once he had lit the field with the Land Rover's headlights. The lads were diving into the snow-filled ditch and disappearing, only to reappear laughing. I tried to chase them but it was almost impossible in the soft snow.

Eventually we all returned to the Land Rover and I jumped into the back with the lads who were all covered in snow and laughing and joking as we returned home. It was lovely and warm indoors after the freezing temperatures outside. The snow and the Land Rover remained for several days and we were out in it every day. Eventually the snow disappeared almost as quickly as it had arrived, but the remains of the snowman were on the lawn for quite a while - the carrot tasted nice! The Land Rover was returned to its owner who lived in Thaxted after Master had cleaned it both inside and out.

The Accident

After my biscuit at Dave and Grace's the rest of the day was fairly quiet. Master spent time digging the piece of ground at the back of the lawn where he grew lots of bits and pieces including carrots, which I thought were delicious. I relaxed on the lawn watching him, it was a beautiful day and the sun was quite warm.

Later in the day after everyone had eaten Master disappeared upstairs only to reappear shortly afterwards in uniform. I got really excited as this could only mean one thing! We went through to the office and he sat down at his desk. As usual I sat on his feet.

Eventually he got up, grabbed some papers and went out through the office door - I followed. We drove around to Dave and Grace's where Dave appeared in his uniform and got into the car with us. Master had explained to me some time ago that Dave was a member of the 'Special Constabulary' whatever that meant. All I knew was that he wore a uniform similar to Master's. I greeted him and then moved to the back shelf. We called at a few houses where the two of them got out and left me guarding the car, then we popped into Saffron Walden Police Station where Master went in alone leaving me and Dave in the car.

Much later we were sitting outside the Guildhall in Thaxted High Street, which was a regular spot for us. A car went past and Master said to Dave "I think we'll have a look at that one" and we pulled out behind it. We followed it up the hill and past the church before it turned off towards Cutlers Green. The roof lights of the police car started flashing and the car ahead pulled over and stopped.

Master got out and walked over to the driver of the car who had also got out. I sat on Dave's lap and watched through the windscreen. The flashing roof lights on our car were reflected in the back window of the car that we had stopped.

Suddenly there was a huge bang from behind and the police car lurched violently forwards and struck the car that we had stopped. Dave's seat had completely collapsed and he was lying flat out on the floor. The force of the crash had catapulted me over Dave's head and onto the back seat, which was badly crushed up from the back. It was just as well that I was not still on Dave's lap as I had been replaced by the entire radio set from the front that had broken away from its mountings in the force of the accident. I leapt down and licked Dave's face and he spoke to me – thankfully he was alright. The back of the police car was smashed in up to the back seats. I heard the car behind revving up and I saw Master running towards us. The car roared past our car and I saw Master stick his arm in the air but the car drove straight at him. At the last second Master leapt out of the way and ended up spread eagled on the path. The car disappeared off towards Cutlers Green with another car following. Master got up and rushed over to us. He tried to open the driver's door but it would only open a small amount. He shouted to Dave who spoke to him as he raised himself off the floor. Master then rushed to a nearby house and returned shortly afterwards. He pulled on the door really hard and it eventually opened enough for us to get out. Dave was a little unsteady on his feet and Master led him to safety.

We then went back outside and Master stopped the next car coming down from the main road. He spoke to the driver who got out then Master and I leapt in it, this was really exciting. There was a strong scent of a dog in the car as we sped off towards Cutlers Green. We went through

Cutlers Green and on towards Debden Green. As we roared down the road I suddenly spotted the rear lights of a car parked on the side of the road. Master slowed down and stopped behind the car, he got out and I followed. There in a ditch on the side of the wide grass verge was a very badly smashed up car on its roof. Nearby there was a rather large lady sitting in the ditch. Initially I could not see what she was sitting on but as we approached it became apparent that she was sitting on someone. A man's head was sticking out from under the woman, his head just above the water, and there were traces of blood on his face. He was shouting, "Get off me". The lady spoke to Master and said "I saw what happened to the police car and I saw him make off so I followed him to here where he swerved off the road and turned the car over in the ditch. He tried to get away after crawling out of the car so I sat on him." At this point a police car arrived, the lady got up and the wet, bedraggled man rose out of the ditch. He appeared to be very unsteady on his feet as he was led away. Master spoke briefly to the lady and we then got back into the car that Master had 'commandeered' and returned to the accident scene where we met Dave, the owner of the car and the driver of the stopped car. Two police cars, an ambulance and a fire engine had joined the chaos; our police car was leaking petrol.

It took ages sorting out the accident. For my safety I was left in a nearby house where I sat with Dave who was being checked over by the ambulance crew. The people in the house gave me a bowl of water and a biscuit, I liked them! I watched out of the sitting room window as a huge lorry arrived and loaded the damaged police car onto it. Master eventually collected me and we got into another police car where Dave was already waiting. We dropped him off at home and returned to the police house and Lyn. Master had a cup of tea and explained to Lyn what had happened, I heard Dave's name mentioned several times. Eventually we all got to bed. I had plenty to dream about that night!!

A Problem in the Office

Master and I had walked Gina to school and I had enjoyed my biscuit with Dave and Grace while Master had a cup of tea. When we got home we found that Lyn had gone out. Master was in the sitting room writing while I curled up at his feet. I went into a deep sleep but my slumbers were rudely interrupted when there was a thunderous bang from the direction of the office. I woke with a start and barked loudly as I ran along the hall to the closed internal office door. Master followed me and as he opened the door the thunderous bang was heard again. Master opened the second door which led into the office. I ran between his legs and up to the glass front office door, barking as I went. I could see a man standing right up against the glass and I jumped back then barked again as he banged on the door. The sound in the office was deafening and his face was right up against the glass.

Master opened the door and the man barged past Master into the office. Master closed the outside door, stepped back behind the counter and closed the counter door down, while the man shouted loudly. Master spoke to the man over the counter, but he continued shouting and waving his arms around. I watched from Master's feet. I started barking at the man, I did not like him. He leaned over the counter and waved his fist at me, I bared my teeth and leapt at him but missed - I ended up in the files under the counter!

Master continued to talk to the man but the man carried on shouting and waving his arms around in a very aggressive manner. I was worried for Master's safety so I started to bark at him again. Master spoke to the man for some time, but the shouting continued. Master raised the counter door, opened the outside door, and beckoned for the man to leave the office.

The man then leapt over the counter and attacked Master with his fists. Master grabbed the phone and dialled but the man grabbed the phone and slammed it down onto the ground, the phone shattered into loads of pieces. Master grabbed the man and slammed him up against the counter. The man tried to swing out against Master but he held his arms down.

A struggle then followed as the man broke Master's grip. He swung wildly at Master but missed every time. I barked and growled at the man and he tried to kick me but I bit his ankle hard. Master had had enough, he took hold of the man's arm as he swung a fist at his face and in an instant the man was on the floor on his face with Master on top of him. The man was shouting and spitting at Master who had him pinned to the floor.

Master remained on top of the man for ages before I heard the sound of sirens approaching and shortly afterwards a number of policemen came rushing into the office through the open door. The man was still struggling as Master got up and the policemen lifted him off the floor. He was kicking and screaming and was soon back on the floor while handcuffs were placed on his wrists. He was then helped to his feet still kicking out at the officers. He was carried screaming and shouting from the office and he was placed into a police van. As the van left the office, a number of policemen came back into the office and Master spoke to them and made cups of tea for everyone. After quite a while the officers left, just as Lyn returned. I had had enough excitement for one day and curled up in my bed, you can guess what I dreamt about.

Three Men in a Wood

Master and I walked Gina to school and I of course had a biscuit or two with Dave and Grace - unfortunately Master collected me before I got my third one. I walked Master back home and he sat and talked to Lyn for some time.

Master and I then went out in the car. We collected Dave, and then went and picked up another friend who I had met on a number of occasions, Arthur Caton, who lived opposite the church. Dave was in the front and I sat on his lap so that I could sit up and watch where we were going. We drove for a short distance and then pulled off the road into the entrance of a wood. Master told me that this was 'West Wood'. I had been in here before some time ago.

We walked off down a track. It was a beautiful day, the sun was shining and there was a strong breeze blowing. As we entered the wood the air was full of strange and interesting scents and sounds worthy of further investigation and I ran on ahead of the men until Master called me back. I returned reluctantly. The men were dawdling along talking but I wanted to go on ahead. A short distance further on I picked up the strong scent of a fox and ran off into the undergrowth under the trees to follow it. Master called me but I ignored him, pretending that I was deaf! Deeper and deeper into the wood I ran and the undergrowth grew less dense as the shade of the trees reduced the light. Master's voice grew fainter the further I ran. Suddenly a new scent crossed my path. This was unusual; it was very musty and even more interesting than the fox. I changed direction and began following this exciting new scent. I ran on for quite a while and I could hear Master's voice getting louder but the scent was growing fainter. I had to make a decision: did I go back to the men or did I continue following the scent? The tone of Master's voice made up my mind and I returned to them. Dave and Arthur were sitting on a bench and Master was standing nearby with his camera. He greeted me and praised me for returning, I liked that.

We stayed there a while and the men talked. I had a game chasing flies in the long grass and jumped back in surprise when a pheasant flew up just in front of me. It flew over me and Master, calling angrily as it disappeared over the trees and out of sight. Dave and Arthur were laughing, as they rose off the seat with a little persuasion from me.

We left the clearing and went back under the trees. The breeze was rustling the leaves which were falling off the trees onto the ground below - one just missed my nose. The path in places was very overgrown where the sunlight pierced through the leaf canopy, Master and the others were alright with their long legs but it was difficult for me with my short ones. Eventually we were back under the trees and the undergrowth died away. As we walked I suddenly spotted a deer ahead of us, standing within the trees. It appeared to spot us at the same time and it ran off, I gave chase despite Master's protestations. The deer moved really fast and had rapidly disappeared. I tried to track it but soon gave up and returned to the men who all greeted me. I stayed with them as we walked on. Suddenly I picked up the unusual scent that I had found earlier on the fox trail and this time it was really strong. I was about to run off and investigate when I think Master must have read my mind and my lead was put on, I was really disappointed!

We then left the path and followed a narrow, but well worn, track through the trees. To my surprise the scent was getting stronger and stronger. I was straining at the lead to go off and investigate but Master held me firm. Dave and Arthur were behind and were keeping very quiet, Master wasn't saying anything either. A little further on we came across a group of large holes in the ground and the scent was everywhere. Outside the holes were heaps of soil and two of the holes had large balls of dried grass outside. I wanted to go down one but I was held firm. Master pointed to the holes but did not say anything. Neither Dave nor Arthur spoke, they just stood there looking. As the breeze dropped all three men crept nearer to the holes and my lead was shortened so that Master was holding me close to him. As I stood there I became aware of a curious noise coming from the huge hole nearest to us. It was a muffled sound that sounded similar to the noise that Master made when he fell asleep with me on his lap - I believe it is called 'snoring'. We stood in silence for a long time listening to the noise, all three men were smiling. Eventually we crept away and it was obvious that I was not going to be allowed to investigate these holes that I later learned were a 'badger sett'. The snoring was coming from the badgers that inhabited the sett.

We returned home and the three men sat in the garden drinking tea and talking while I sat on Dave's feet, thirsty and tired. Lyn filled my water bowl and after a good drink I went to sleep on the grass in the sun, dreaming of trees, foxes and other things.

A Walk on the Motorway

Early one morning Gina and I were bundled into the car with some luggage and before we knew it we were off. I had the back seat all to myself - Master and Gina were in the front talking. I was soon sound asleep.

I awoke with a start as familiar scents drifted into the car and I sat up and looked out of the window. I could see hills all around us with sheep on - we were up on the Downs again. I whined at Master as I needed the toilet and we pulled off the road into a grassy area at the bottom of a hill and stopped the car. Gina opened her door to let me squeeze through the gap between the seats. I climbed over Gina's lap and took a giant leap out of the car onto the soft grass that was full of scents. I soon forgot all about my toilet as the scents were a lot more interesting! I followed one and then another, there were so many to choose from. Master got out and spoke to me and the tone of his voice indicated that he was not happy. I did my toilet and reluctantly got back into the car. I sat up on the back seat watching as we drove off.

Shortly afterwards we were back in Worthing and parked outside a house that I recognised. We all got out and went indoors; I was given a bowl of water as it was really hot, while Master unloaded the bags and cases out of the car. Gina was very excited as she spoke to a woman who Master had told me was his 'mother'. We stayed there quite a while and everybody was talking. Eventually Master and I were back in the car while Gina and Master's mother waved at us as we drove off.

We were soon back up on the Downs and after turning off the main road we travelled along a narrow road for quite a while. I was really excited as I sat up in the front seat, I could sense we were going for a walk. We parked up and as Master opened his door I ran across his lap in my excitement and leapt out of the door. Master grabbed his camera and we were off. There was a strong breeze blowing and the air was full of scents.

We were at Cissbury Ring and we climbed the hill to the very top - it was beautiful. Birds were singing in the clear sky above us, Master told me they were skylarks. He sat down on the grass at the top and I sat on his lap surveying the landscape below us then he lay back on to the soft grass and I licked his face, he laughed when his beard made me sneeze.

We stayed up on the hill for quite a while but eventually climbed down and returned to the car. We drove off and I lay on the front seat and slept. There was a nice breeze coming in from Master's open window and even the noise of the traffic didn't keep me awake.

However after travelling for quite a while I became aware that we had been stopped for some time and there was no sound of traffic. I sat up in the seat and looked out to find that there were loads of cars in front of us. Master looked down at me as I looked at him. He told me that this was a 'traffic jam' whatever that was. I did not like it, there was no fresh air coming into the car and it was really hot. Master switched the engine off and sat there tapping his fingers on the steering wheel. He wound down my window and I sniffed the air but there were no scents apart from hot tarmac. There were vehicles all around including a huge coach right behind us. Master was talking to the driver of the car next to us through the open windows. I was suddenly startled and barked loudly as a man walked past my window, Master told me to "be quiet". After a while there were a lot of people walking around outside, so Master put my lead on and led me out. Walking between the cars was quite interesting - I only wished that I was taller! I went to the toilet behind a towering lorry and we then walked back to the coach behind our car. Master spoke to the driver who produced a bowl of cool water for me and Master was also given a drink.

We then went for another walk between the cars which wasn't without its difficulties as drivers had their doors open. People were standing around talking in the searing heat, even the road surface was really hot on my feet. There were no vehicles at all on the other carriageway. As we walked Master explained to me that this was the M25 motorway and that it was closed as a 'war time bomb had been dug up at the QE2 bridge works at the Dartford crossing' - of course as usual I hadn't a clue what he meant! We returned to the coach and Master sat on the step in the shade with me on his lap. He spoke for quite a while to the driver and had another drink. My bowl was refilled and I emptied it again. Several other people joined us and were given drinks by the coach driver. The coach itself had been empty but we went on board and sat in the front seat opposite the driver and a number of other people, including some children, joined us on board. It was cooler on board than outside but I was still panting heavily. The children came up and stroked and made a fuss of me, which I liked, they were nice children.

The hours went by and more and more people received drinks from the coach driver. A police vehicle stopped on the opposite carriageway and a number of policemen got out, stepped over the metal barrier and started to spread out and talk to groups of people who were standing around. One policeman came on board the coach and spoke to everyone on board. There were a number of groans which suggested to me that it was not good news.

Master and I went for another walk and I had a toilet. We went back to our car and got in then Master moved his seat right back and laid down as far as he could. I jumped up on to his lap and put my head out of the window, there was an eerie silence outside. I curled up and went to sleep between the steering wheel and Master's head.

I awoke sometime later to the sound of traffic thundering past outside. Master woke at the same time. It was getting dark and the cars in the opposite carriageway had their lights on. Master sat up, almost squashing me against the wheel, for which he apologised as he placed me down on the seat. I sat up and looked out of the window; there was still no movement on our side of the road. Master put my lead on and we got out. The sound of the traffic was quite frightening as it thundered by so close to us but at least it was a little cooler. I did my toilet and we eventually ended up back on the coach where Master spoke to the coach driver, who made a fuss of me, I liked him too!

Eventually lights appeared on our carriageway way ahead of us. We climbed out of the coach and got back into the car. Master started the engine and after a few minutes we were off with all the other cars, albeit very slowly. We passed through a long tunnel and it was a slow journey home but eventually we turned into the rear yard of the police house. The moon was high in the sky as we got out and Lyn came and greeted us. I slept well that night - I had plenty to dream about - not every Jack Russell can say that they had walked down the 'M25'!!

The Snake

One morning I collected my biscuits from Dave and Grace whilst Master took Gina to school, then we went for a long walk down along the river. However, instead of walking towards Piggotts Hill and home, we went off towards Yardley Hall. It was a beautiful, warm, sunny day and we were walking along a field track with a hedge on one side when a rabbit suddenly came out of the hedge and ran flat out away from us along the track. I gave chase but it rapidly vanished into the tall wheat in the field and although I followed I could not pick up its scent, I soon returned to Master.

We followed the track around a corner, past a small wood and down a slope towards the river. I ran on ahead of Master investigating all manner of scents when suddenly I spotted a curious shape coiled up on the dirt track ahead of me. I stopped abruptly and sniffed the air desperately seeking any scent from the object but there was none. I stood very still as I was not at all certain about this strange object and something inside me was telling me that it was dangerous.

I heard Master approaching from behind and this gave me the courage to creep forward very slowly towards the object. I kept my head down, sniffing the ground to read any scents that might indicate what it was and whether it was edible! I was only a short distance from it when suddenly a head appeared from within the coil and a tongue flicked out of its mouth, it was alive! I jumped back straight into Master's legs. Master told me that it was a snake and as he spoke to me the snake slid off down the track towards the river.

Seizing the advantage I chased after it but was stopped in my tracks as it turned and reared up. I started barking excitedly but the snake took little notice of me before sliding off again towards the river. Giving it a very wide berth I ran around the snake, barking at it. I was now ahead of it but I didn't know if that was a good place to be. However my immediate danger was averted when the snake changed course and slid off into the short grass on the side of the track - the river was only a few feet away.

The snake ignored my barks and on reaching the river bank it slid down onto the surface of the water and swam quickly across to the other side. I leapt in after it but by the time I started to swim the snake had disappeared. I hunted around for it in the bank-side undergrowth but there was no sign of it. Master called me back and I returned and shook myself next to him; the tone of his voice said it all. I was not really sure what to make of snakes - a creature that leaves no scent is an oddity to me.

Banjo

It was that time of year again when stirrings deep within me turned my thoughts to finding a mate. One morning, after my visit to Dave and Grace, Master and I walked down Park Street to a cottage next door to Park Farm where Master knocked on the door. I became excited when I heard a dog barking from within and by the tone it sounded like a Jack Russell. The door eventually opened and a very scruffy, long-haired, black and white Jack Russell came bounding out. We greeted each other and played chase around the small garden. I learnt that his name was Banjo. He kept on sniffing my rear end which I did not take too kindly to and I told him so in no uncertain terms. I did not like all his attentions and eventually I snapped at him and nipped him on the nose He jolted back with a startled 'yelp', I had had enough. I think Master sensed this for he gathered me up, spoke briefly to the dog's owner and we left. I walked Master home and he did not speak to me all the way - obviously I was in the 'dog house' again.

A few days passed and the yearnings inside grew stronger and stronger. One morning there was a knock at the front door. I barked and ran to the frosted glass door - I could see someone standing there with a dog and I got very excited. Lyn opened the door and I recognised Banjo immediately. He led his owner through the hall after we had greeted each other we went out into the back garden where we were joined by Master. We ran around the garden where Banjo kept sniffing my rear end again and once or twice tried to climb on my back but I was having none of that. I snapped at him hard but he would not take the hint, he continued chasing me.

The two Masters were standing outside the kitchen door, talking and drinking tea. I was really getting fed up with Banjo and eventually ran over to Master and sat between his legs looking up at him anxiously. I was hoping that he would pick me up but he didn't, in fact he totally ignored me and my problems. Banjo came over to me so I moved between Master's legs and snarled at him. He ignored me then tried to mount me again. That was the last straw - I turned on him and bit him on the nose. He jumped back with a loud yelp, which attracted the two men's attention. Master reached down and picked me up - boy was I glad of that - Banjo was also gathered up. We faced each other whilst the men talked briefly then Banjo and his Master left the garden via the back gate. I was in the dog house that night.

I never saw Banjo again and I never raised a family.

Marc

Marc had been living with us for a long time and I had got used to the regular walks with him, Phil and the lads. He and Phil shared the front bedroom along with any of their mates that decided to stay. I liked the lads - they always made a fuss of me once I had approved of them staying. Sometimes it was quite late when they came in but once I was satisfied that I knew who they were I allowed them upstairs.

One morning Marc crept into the office when Master had not noticed and picked up Master's camera that was on his desk. I was lying in the hall by the front door underneath where the coats hung. Both the office doors were wedged open which had become the norm. Marc called me and I looked up, then I heard the camera click. Marc then put the camera back on the desk and crept back out of the office, patting me on the head as he passed me.

But one night events occurred that were to change our lives forever. Master and Lyn were watching TV and I was sitting on Lyn's feet. Later there was a knock at the door and I jumped up and barked loudly. Master went to the front door and opened it. In came Gerry who I recognised and Marc and Phil came down from upstairs. The lads spoke to Master who then went to his car - I followed. We all got into the car with me sitting on Marc's lap, and we drove off. We drove down to the other end of the town, where we stopped outside a pub and the lads got out. After they had spoken briefly to Master we left them and drove back to the house where I returned to Lyn's feet. Later Master and Lyn went to bed and I curled up in my basket and slept, all was quiet in the house.

Much later the peace was shattered when the lads returned home. They were talking and laughing as they came in and when I greeted them they patted me. I returned to my basket as they disappeared upstairs though I could still hear them whispering in their room. Eventually the house returned to peace and quiet.

However, some time later I was awoken by a loud commotion from upstairs. There was a lot of screaming and shouting. Lyn came running downstairs and went into the sitting room, grabbing the phone. She appeared very distressed and she sat on the settee talking frantically to someone. I heard Master shouting "Marc, Marc, come on Marc". The tone of Master's voice frightened me and I ran upstairs to see what was happening. I passed Phil coming down and he was very upset. He gathered me up off the stairs and brought me back downstairs.

I sat in the sitting room on Phil's lap while Lyn was back on the phone again, I could not understand what was going on. There was a loud bang on the front door and I ran to the door barking. Phil followed me and opened the door. Two men in uniform came in - there was an ambulance parked outside with its roof lights flashing. The men spoke briefly to Phil and then rushed upstairs. I was about to follow but Lyn scooped me up and I sat on her lap on the settee. Phil and Gina were sitting next to us and everyone seemed very anxious. I could hear lots of strange noises coming from upstairs along with Master's voice, which sounded very upset.

There was another loud knock at the door and Lyn answered it to let a lady in - she was a doctor who I recognised as she had visited the office before and spoken to Master. She went upstairs and soon afterwards Master and Gerry came down, they both appeared very upset. I jumped up on to Gerry's lap and licked his hand then I heard the bedroom door shut. We all sat in the sitting room.

Soon after there was a third knock at the door. Master opened it and there was a second much larger ambulance with its roof lights flashing. Two more men in uniform came in and rushed up the stairs. Master and Lyn stood at the bottom of the stairs anxiously looking up. Another knock at the door admitted two policemen who briefly spoke to Master and then went upstairs. Master and Lyn returned to the sitting room where Phil, Gerry and Gina were sitting.

Eventually the lady doctor came down the stairs and spoke to Lyn and Master, who were by this time extremely upset. Phil, Gina and Gerry went over the road to Andy's parent's house. Two men came down the stairs carrying a narrow bed covered over with a blanket. I sniffed at the bed when the men reached the bottom of the stairs and found that Marc was under the blanket. We all stood in the porch of the front door as Marc went into the big ambulance. Moments later one of the men called to Master and Lyn who went over to the ambulance and spoke briefly to them. Master then gathered Phil and Gerry who were standing outside. Master picked me up and we all climbed into the ambulance where Marc was laying. I looked down at him; I couldn't understand what was happening. Master said something and we all then left the ambulance. The ambulance with Marc then left and this was the last time I was to see him. Master sat in the office with me and the two police officers for quite a while. Eventually they left and Master lifted me up onto his lap stroking me gently. He told me that Marc had died and he was only twenty one. For once I think I understood what he meant.

No one went to bed. Lyn spent a long time on the phone, several people arrived and sat with Lyn and Master. Later in the morning John and Kath arrived and other people came and went throughout the day. Master and Lyn remained in the sitting room for most of the day. Phil and Gina returned to the house in the evening and John and Kath left fairly late.

Although everyone went to bed relatively early Master and Lyn came down quite regularly through the night and sat in the sitting room. The following morning I took Master for a walk as it was a lovely sunny day with a gentle breeze blowing and we went down to the river. Master spoke very little as we walked slowly along and I stayed close to him. We walked across the little footbridge over the river then along to Piggots Hill and back to the house. When we got back John and Kath had arrived.

With Marc gone the house seemed very quiet and it was a long time before any form of normality returned.

New Surroundings

Quite a while after Marc's death more events were to occur which were to change my life forever.

One day Master loaded up the car with boxes and cases and my basket. I was bundled into the car and we drove a short distance to a house that Master told me was called 'Pandemonium'. Pat was there - I knew her and her dog 'Chela' who was a large black Labrador bitch. The car was unloaded and my basket was placed in the kitchen next to Chela's. Chela and I greeted each other and after we had sniffed each other all over we settled down in front of the open fire which was lovely and warm. It was that time of the year when the funny tree with lights all over it was in the house. Much later we settled down in the kitchen, Chela in her basket and me in mine, but after a while I climbed in with Chela who was lovely and warm. It did seem strange sharing a bed with another dog and it took a while to get used to.

The following morning Chela and I had a little dispute as to whose bowl of food was whose, but we soon sorted that out. I got told off by Master although I did not think it was really fair, just because I wanted both bowls, I couldn't see what was wrong with that! I hadn't had to share before and it was going to take some getting used to.

Master and Pat took us both for a walk through the fields behind the house. It was great having company on the walk. Chela and I ran along the path leading to a wood. We started chasing each other but Chela was much bigger than me and could cover a lot more ground than my short little legs, still it was great fun. Just before we reached the wood

Chela spooked a hare in the field and the chase was on. Chela was running a lot faster than me but even so neither of us was any match for the hare that soon disappeared. Chela continued running but I couldn't see the point and I returned to Master. Eventually Chela returned panting heavily and covered in mud but without the hare of course.

Life was very different where I was now living but Chela and I soon became great pals. On our walks we developed a system of hunting which proved to be very effective. Because of my small size I would hunt along the base of the ditches flushing out any creature in there. Chela would remain at the top of the bank on the path and chase anything that came out - she never caught any of the creatures but it was great fun. On one occasion I did catch a rat and with a quick flick its neck was broken. Master was impressed and patted me. He tried to get me to drop it but I wouldn't - this was my prize. Chela sniffed my catch and I carried it all the way home but Master was not at all happy as we walked into the back garden, and he would not open the back door of the house for us until I was persuaded to drop my catch. In we went and Chela and I curled up in the basket and slept. We had had a busy and exciting day. Later I went outside to inspect my catch but it was gone.

Cassie to the Rescue

One morning, after breakfast and the shortest of walks, we were bundled into the car and we were off. Chela and I were in the back of Pat's car watching the traffic behind. After a while it became obvious that this was going to be a long journey so we settled down and slept.

Much later Chela woke with a start, which in turn woke me up. She had recognised a scent that had drifted into the car and she became very excited and restless. Soon after this we turned off the main road and travelled slowly down a very narrow lane and through a gateway with a huge tree to one side. Chela by this time was going berserk - so was I because I needed to go to the toilet! We stopped and were let out, there were interesting scents everywhere. We were met by a man and woman who I later learnt from Master were Pat's parents, Peter and Val.

Chela and I went for a walk around the huge garden and there were scents everywhere. I saw a strange creature with a large bushy tail and I gave chase but it scampered up the large tree near the entrance. Chela and I watched it disappear in the leaf cover high above us - Chela was really excited and was barking loudly. Master told me that it was a squirrel. Eventually we were beckoned in doors as darkness fell.

We slept well in the kitchen as Master and Pat had brought our beds down but we woke early and Chela started barking for breakfast. Peter came down first and we greeted him. Pat soon followed and we had our breakfast. Master and Val were last and we were banished to our beds whilst the humans ate.

Later we watched as Master put on his coat and boots and grabbed our leads, we both got really excited as we followed him out into the garden. We had a quick run around the garden before our leads were put on and we were led out of the front gate and down the hill. At the bottom we turned left out of the lane and went up into the woodland that Master told me was called Ashdown Forest.

There was a lot of deep, dead bracken and undergrowth which was great for hunting and the air was full of damp, musky scent. There had been a sharp frost overnight and the bracken was draped in cobwebs that were covered in frost and glistened in the sunlight. The spiders however had not bargained on us two hooligans!

We walked for ages and went past a pond that Master told me was a 'dew pond' - Chela and I decided to have a dip and though the water was really cold we didn't mind. We eventually came out and shook ourselves next to Master and by the tone of his voice he was not happy so we ran off back into the undergrowth. Chela was carrying a large stick that she had retrieved from the pond. She brought it back to Master on a number of occasions and he threw it deep into the undergrowth so she could fetch it. I couldn't be bothered with that so I concentrated on investigating the undergrowth.

Eventually we started to head back to the house and found ourselves in a very overgrown field leading to the lane and the house beyond. Chela had run on ahead after her stick that Master had thrown. Suddenly two huge dogs appeared from nowhere and immediately went after Chela. She went down submissively, obviously very frightened by the onslaught from the two dogs. They stood over her in a threatening manner with bared teeth, snarling at her. I could see that my pal was in serious trouble and I was having none of that. I rushed over to her defence, barking at the two dogs that towered over me. I bit one in the back leg as he went to run off, then I set on the other one that had decided to challenge me, but a hard bite on his side sent him running after his companion. I gave chase after both of them, biting the slower of the two on the back of his leg which brought forth a loud yelp as they disappeared through a deep hedge.

I did not follow and the two dogs did not reappear. I returned to Chela who was quite shaken. I licked her face and she rose to her feet. Master was standing near the gate to the field. He greeted us both and patted me on the head saying "Good girl, well done". Chela and I walked home with our heads held high.

A Romp on the Bed

Often in the mornings Pat would come down first and let us out into the garden before giving us our breakfast. Afterwards Chela and I would sometimes sneak upstairs to where Master was sound asleep in bed. I would sneak into the bed, creep down under the duvet and snuggle up against Master's legs, it was lovely and warm under the covers.

One day I had done this as normal and the next thing I knew was that there was a huge thump on the bed. Master awoke with a shout and there then followed a series of jumps on the bed near me. I started growling as Chela tried to jump on me. Master was in hysterics as I moved slowly around, out of sight of Chela who continued jumping. Master eventually persuaded her to get off the bed and I was also ejected.

This became a regular game in the mornings and sometimes we were allowed to go to sleep on and in the bed, which was a real treat.

The Deer

After breakfast one morning Master placed our collars on and put his boots on - this was the signal that we were going for a walk and we both got really excited. We were pulling hard on the leads as we left the house and entered the fields behind the house - Master would not walk fast enough! The first field was full of long grass and a regular dog walking spot. There were interesting dog scents everywhere and we met 'Charlie', another Jack Russell, taking his Lyn for a walk. We greeted each other while Master spoke to the lady. Chela started pulling hard on her lead and we were soon on our way again. Once in the second field heading for Copthall Wood we were off our leads and away. It was a beautiful morning, the sun was high in the sky and there was a gentle breeze. On and on we went past Copthall and Blunts Wood where Chela got really excited when she found a fresh fox scent. We followed it for some time but eventually Master called us back.

As we were about to leave Blunts Wood Chela picked up another interesting scent which sent her scurrying off at a full run, I followed. Down a bank we ran and through a gap in a hedge. There on the other side, just a little further along the hedge, standing in the field in the sun was a group of deer. Our sudden appearance startled them and they ran off along the line of the hedge - we immediately gave chase. Chela was soon well ahead of me as the deer disappeared through the hedge and into the wood. Chela was not gaining on them at all and I certainly wasn't. Chela was barking excitedly as she crashed through the undergrowth. I heard Master calling us but ignored him, this was much more fun. We were by now simply following the deer's scent as they were long gone. We had travelled the full length of the wood and had come out into the bright sunlight at the end. There was no sign of the deer. I could hear Master's voice faintly in the distance so we reluctantly re-entered the wood and eventually returned to him.

We continued on our walk, panting heavily after the chase. A little further on I had gone down into a ditch covered in bramble. It was quite dark within and I was moving slowly along when I suddenly picked up the scent of something ahead of me. I moved quickly along the base of the dry ditch when suddenly I saw the object of my attentions. It saw me at the same time and ran off along the ditch, it was a Muntjack Deer. I barked loudly to warn Chela, but she was already aware and was running along the top of the bank. The deer disappeared from my view as it ran up the bank in a clearing of bramble. By the time I reached the top of the bank the deer and Chela were nowhere to be seen. I followed Chela's scent through a hedge and there, way off in the distance, was my pal running flat out, but I couldn't see the deer. I ran after her as she disappeared through a hedge on the other side of the field. I found Chela casting around in a big circle trying to pick up the scent of the deer, but without success. Way off in the distance Master was calling us and after another unsuccessful cast for the scent we ran back to him. This was turning into an interesting, if not exhausting, walk.

The journey home was via a different route, with plenty more ditches to explore. In one a pheasant got up and Chela gave chase but as I reached the top the bird was disappearing over a wood and Chela was soon on her way back to me. We were both worn out when we got back. Chela and I slept for the rest of the day in the sitting room in the sun.

Chela and I were to have many adventures involving deer, foxes, rabbits, hares, pheasants, dogs, and of course cats and rats - the last two I certainly did not like, and Chela was not too keen either, especially on cats!

Hare Coursing

One morning I was up bright and early, Chela stayed in bed as she was not at all well. She had been unwell for the past few days and I tried to rouse her but she did not want to know. Pat let me out into the garden as Master appeared in uniform.

Soon after breakfast there was a knock at the door. I barked and ran to answer it and Master followed me to open the door. There was a policeman standing there who I recognized as Trevor. I jumped up - I could smell dog on his uniform - and Master told me firmly to get down. Trevor came in and they spoke for a while then Master grabbed his coat and opened the door. Not to be outdone, I ran between his and Trevor's legs and ran up to the huge police vehicle parked outside. Master opened the door and I was in like a shot. There was no back shelf here so I sat up on the back seat.

We called in at Saffron Walden Police Station where I was left guarding the vehicle but within a short time we were back on the road with Trevor driving. We went right out into the country and simply drove slowly around the lanes. We stopped on top of a hill in a large gravel area and there was a spectacular view in all directions. Master let me out and I went off to investigate some interesting scents. It was a beautiful sunny day and there were birds singing high in the clear sky above us. I watched one come gliding down fast and land in the field near to me - Master called them skylarks. Master and Trevor were talking in the vehicle with the doors open.

I was just about to investigate an interesting fresh rat scent in a small hole in a bank near the vehicle when the police radio burst into life and Trevor spoke on it. Immediately Master called me back to the vehicle and I jumped in. We were straight off, racing down the lanes. Master was looking into a field on his side and I looked as well. The vehicle came to an abrupt halt when a line of men came into view way off in the middle of a huge field. Each was holding a greyhound on a lead and two men were walking ahead of the main line with greyhounds by their sides.

As we watched I suddenly saw a hare bolt off immediately in front of the two men. They slipped the leads off their dogs who were at full speed within seconds. The hare was jinking its run and was easily gaining on the dogs. Master spoke to Trevor and we started moving off down the lane. The men in the field looked towards us and immediately started running. We accelerated away and came down to a small crossroads where we turned in the direction of the men. A little further along were three cars parked up in a gateway to the field. The men were still some way off and were running towards the cars. The two greyhounds chasing the hare were running up a hill with the hare way ahead of them. As Master and Trevor got out a second police car arrived and stopped as the ten men arrived at their cars. I was watching the greyhounds - they were all panting heavily and were covered in mud, as were the men.

I squeezed through to the front of the vehicle and watched what was going on, as I was nice and high up I could see everything. Master was talking to one man who was taller than him and a lot bigger. The man started shouting at Master, I could hear him from where I was. I started barking - no one shouts at my Master! The man was waving his arms around and he took a lunge at Master. The next thing I knew was that the man was on the ground with

Master on top of him. He was putting those strange things that he once told me were 'handcuffs' onto the man's wrists. Trevor had rushed over and assisted as the man started struggling. Once handcuffed the man was dragged to his feet by Master and Trevor and was placed in the back of our vehicle. I stayed on the front seat and glared at him, I did not like him. He remained quiet. A huge police van then arrived and the other men were bundled into it with their greyhounds, one in particular was a very handsome dog. I watched him with interest as he jumped into the van, but unfortunately he did not see me and I did not see him again.

Trevor and Master returned to our vehicle and Master got in the back while Trevor drove again. The handcuffed man remained very quiet on the journey to Saffron Walden Police Station where all the men in the van were being escorted into the station in a line - they were all wearing handcuffs. I was hoping to see the dog again but they all remained in the van. We sat in the car for quite a while, but after a brief radio message Trevor and Master got out and helped the man out. They walked him to the back door of the building, Master on one side and Trevor on the other, and then disappeared inside and I settled down to guard the car. It was a long time before they returned without the man, it was dark and I awoke from a deep sleep as the door opened.

Trevor drove us home and I was soon sitting in front of the fire. Master explained to me that the men had been 'hare coursing' illegally, whatever that meant? All I knew was that there were some handsome dogs that went hare coursing! Chela was feeling a lot better and curled up with me in front of the fire. I slept well that night after all the excitement.

The Hunt

Early one morning Master came down in uniform and soon after breakfast there was a knock at the door. I barked and Chela and I raced to the front door. Master opened it and there was Trevor standing outside. He came in and Master spoke to him. As they went to leave Chela and I rushed between their legs and jumped into the back of the huge police vehicle. We settled down as Trevor drove off.

After a short drive we stopped on the forecourt of a Public House and parked. Trevor and Master talked in the front while Chela and I watched out of the windows. There were a few horses with riders on board on the road in front of us, and as we watched more and more horses began to arrive. Some of the riders dismounted and went into the pub. Before long it was packed outside with horses and people on foot. Trevor and Master got out with their high hats on and went onto the road where cars appeared to be having difficulty getting through. Master and Trevor got between the horses and helped the cars to pass.

Suddenly, as if from nowhere, a pack of hounds appeared in front of the police vehicle and two riders who were mounted nearby were cracking whips. The hounds responded by gathering together close to these riders. A strange sound then pierced the air as one of the riders blew into a strange contraption. Immediately afterwards the two men rode off down the road with the hounds following and all the horses following along behind. Chela could not contain her excitement any longer and barked out loud, which was quite deafening in the vehicle. Master came back to the car and told her to "be quiet", his tone meant more to us than what he said and she soon shut up.

Eventually Master and Trevor came back and got in (after I had squeezed to the rear seat with Chela who was still very excited). We drove off and soon afterwards we came up behind the horses and followed them for a while until the horses turned off the lane into a field on a hill. We travelled past the horses and continued up the lane to the top where we turned off into a farm track and stopped. Way below us I could see the hounds working through a clump of trees with some low undergrowth. The horses were standing near the roadside hedge. Chela and I were watching intently out of the window while Master and Trevor were talking.

Suddenly I heard a hound bark and almost at the same time a large fox came running out of the cover towards us. The hounds were soon chasing the fox towards us and the horses were galloping up behind them. Chela started barking excitedly and jumped up at the window, pushing me over. Master told her to "be quiet" but she ignored him and continued barking. The fox turned across the field towards a hedge and the hounds followed in full cry with the horses galloping after the hounds. I joined Chela in barking at the exciting spectacle in front of us. Master and Trevor got out of the vehicle and stood nearby, leaving us to guard the vehicle.

The fox disappeared through the hedge closely followed by the hounds. The horses went down the line of the hedge until they reached a gap where they all jumped through. As the last horse was disappearing through the gap the fox reappeared through the hedge further down and ran past the horse, the rider appearing to be unaware of the fox being so close. The fox ran up the hedge towards us but there were no hounds behind it. Master and Trevor stood very still as the fox approached. The animal ran between the two men and disappeared under the police vehicle. Chela and I ran to the other side of the back seat to see where the fox had gone and we saw it run into a dense bush by the side of the vehicle. Chela continued to bark loudly and there was still no sign of the hounds.

Some time later the hounds appeared back through the hedge and started running around in the field with their noses to the ground. Suddenly one hound gave out a loud cry and immediately started to run towards us, the others followed. Trevor and Master got back in to the vehicle as the hounds arrived. They were all very muddy and panting heavily. The hounds ran around the vehicle as the riders arrived and I jumped back when one leapt up at the window and we both barked. It left muddy smears on the glass as it jumped down. The riders with the whips cracked them loudly and the hounds gathered around them. They were then led out of the field into the lane and the horses followed. After they were gone we were allowed out of the car for a toilet while Trevor and Master sat talking and laughing.

Soon after we got back into the car I suddenly saw the fox again on the track ahead of us. It leapt out of the hedge, walked down the hedge past the gap that the horses had used, walked down to the trees and the cover where it first appeared and then vanished. Master and Trevor were still laughing.

Eventually we drove out of the field and along the lane and caught up with the hunt, who were riding along a lane towards a large wood. We turned off the lane into a field with the trees on the other side. We had a good view as the hounds entered. Two men on horses were standing back from the wood in the field. Trevor and Master got out but we were told to "stay", which we reluctantly did (we had no choice really as the doors were slammed shut!) I squeezed through to the front seat and sat up to watch while Chela watched from the back. The main group of horses was standing in the corner of the field.

Nothing happened for what seemed to be ages until suddenly a fox came running out of the hedge between the two riders and ran straight towards us. The two riders started calling and waved their riding hats in the air and this seemed to spur our 'cousin' on even more. It turned across in front of us and disappeared through the hedge. Almost immediately a second fox appeared and ran in the opposite direction towards the gathered horses. Several riders were calling and the fox turned across in front of them and bolted through the hedge nearby.

As if that was not enough for the hounds to chase, almost immediately after the second fox disappeared a herd of six deer came crashing out of the wood running at speed past the two riders and across the field ahead of us. The hounds then appeared in full cry after the deer. Chela and I began barking excitedly - we wanted to join in. The two riders with whips then came out of the wood and began to ride at speed after the hounds, cracking their whips and blowing the strange horn. I assumed that they were trying to get the hounds under control but the hounds were not having any of it. The deer crashed through the hedge and were soon followed by the hounds. The two riders could not get through so they galloped up the field and past us, speaking briefly to Master and Trevor. They rode out onto the lane followed by the rest of the horses. Trevor and Master got back in the car and Master placed me back on the rear seat with Chela. After the last horse was well clear of the gate we pulled out and followed the horses.

We travelled for quite a distance behind the horses until they eventually turned off the lane into a huge field of stubble, whereupon they all burst into a gallop to the other side of the field and then stood in a corner. I could not see the hounds. We all got out and flasks and sandwiches appeared - we were given a bowl of water - this hunting lark is thirsty work. Master gave us half each of one of his sandwiches and Trevor gave us some tit bits as well - I could get to enjoy following the hunt! I investigated some interesting scents along a nearby hedge, including a fairly fresh fox scent; one had been along here quite recently. Trevor and Master were talking as they ate their food and Chela stayed near Master - she was hoping for more food.

We had been there for quite a while, when the peace and tranquility was suddenly shattered. A group of young men and women suddenly appeared in the field from the other end of the roadside hedge. They were shouting and calling as they began to run across the field towards the horses which were still gathered in the far corner. Trevor and Master got into the police vehicle and Chela and I were rapidly bundled into the back. We set off across the field at high speed and we bounced around on the back seat.

We managed to intercept the group before they reached the horses and they stopped running. Master and Trevor got out and spoke to the group who were all covered in mud. Two of the men had very long hair and others were wearing something that covered their heads, only showing their eyes and mouth - I did not like this and Chela started barking at them. Eventually they turned around and walked back towards the gateway from where they had appeared. Trevor got back into the car and began to follow them speaking briefly on the radio. Master was walking. Two of the group continued shouting and calling as they turned and looked at the horses in the distance.

It was a long way back to the lane but eventually we were there. The group got into a big van and Master rejoined us. He spoke on the radio briefly as the van moved off and we followed - boy this was exciting! Very shortly afterwards we were joined by a second police vehicle with two police officers on board. Master tried to explain to us that the people in the van were 'hunt saboteurs' whatever that meant, all I knew was that I did not like them very much.

We followed the van for some distance before it stopped in a field gateway and two occupants jumped out and stood in the field, looking. Master got out and stood nearby. The two then ran back to the van and it turned around in the gateway and drove off back the way we had come. Trevor turned our vehicle around as Master leapt in, slipping slightly on the step as he did so. We followed the van and the other police vehicle followed on behind us. As we reached the field where we had left the hunt, the van slowed, for ahead of us were the horses riding along the lane away from us. I suddenly heard the hooter from the van in front. We were travelling very slowly and Master jumped out and went to the driver's door to speak to the driver. Moments later he was back with us.

Eventually the horses turned off the lane and rode up a long concrete track. We followed along with the van. The hounds were a long way ahead of us and I saw them leave the track and go off into some scrub to our side. The van in front emptied out and Master and Trevor got out, as did the two officers behind us. The saboteurs were shouting and calling at the hounds as they disappeared into the dense scrub. The horses rode on up the track away from the van and its occupants, who continued their calls. Master spoke to them again and they did quieten down for a while but soon became as loud as before.

Suddenly two of the saboteurs ran across the field as one of the riders that had followed the hounds into the scrub, reappeared with some of the hounds. They were shouting and screaming at the rider. Master and Trevor ran after them as the others cheered and clapped. Master brought one down by leaping at the saboteur's legs, which was later described as a 'tackle'. Trevor brought the other one down in a similar way. A loud cheer went up from the individuals by the van as their two friends were brought back in handcuffs to the police car behind us. They were placed in the back of the car which then left. Both Master and Trevor were covered in mud from head to foot.

Master spoke briefly on the radio and soon afterwards a police van arrived with two more officers on board. The hounds were still in the scrub and the horses rode off up the concrete track, eventually going out of sight. The remaining saboteurs got into their van and attempted to turn around on the track but the back of the van dropped off the track onto some mud and the wheels started to spin and sink at the same time. All the saboteurs got out, but this did not seem to make any difference and mud was flying everywhere from the rear tyres. They all started pushing from the back, but all that happened was that they all got splattered in mud!

The police van turned around and parked at the entrance to the track. Trevor turned our vehicle around and we returned to the lane and drove off in search of the hunt which we had not seen for some time.

The remainder of the day appeared to be fairly uneventful. We caught brief glimpses of the hounds way off across the fields but there was no more trouble from the saboteurs.

As darkness fell we called in at Saffron Walden Police Station and as we parked I saw the two saboteurs that Master and Trevor had caught earlier leaving the station with papers in their hands. Almost immediately their van appeared, still covered in mud, and the two got in the back before it drove off. Trevor and Master went into the station, leaving us guarding the vehicle.

They reappeared, laughing, some time later and Trevor dropped Master and us dogs off at home. Pat laughed when she saw the state of Master but Chela and I were nice and clean. We slept well that night, dreaming of foxes, horses, hounds, saboteurs, and of course Master covered in mud.

Life Goes On

Pat and Master's house is called 'Pandemonium' and it has always lived up to its name - life has never been dull. Wildlife of all shapes and sizes still arrive at our door. The downstairs toilet, which is next to the front door, is always out of bounds to us as there are often creatures in there. The problem for me was that our food sack was also kept in there! A tawny owl nearly attacked me once as I sneaked in there one evening to try and steal a morsel, which I must confess I had done before. I was not aware of the bird sitting above me on a shoe shelf. It flew down and just missed my head as I quickly pulled back. Food was a big driving force in me but not worth getting hooked by a talon for.

Chela and I were to have many more adventures and fun together. We did have our occasional differences of opinion and these were normally over food, but we always made up and curled up together at the end of the day.

Life goes on.